STORIES BY SERGIO TRONCOSO

A PECULIAR KIND OF IMMIGRANT'S SON

STORIES BY SERGIO TRONCOSO

A PECULIAR KIND OF IMMIGRANT'S SON

CINCO PUNTOS PRESS
www.cincopuntos.com

FIRST EDITION
10 9 8 7 6 5 4 3 2 1

Library of Congress Cataloging-in-Publication Data

Names: Troncoso, Sergio, 1961- author.
Title: A peculiar kind of immigrant's son / short stories by Sergio Troncoso.
Description: First edition. | El Paso, Texas : Cinco Puntos Press, [2019]
Identifiers: LCCN 2019009976 | ISBN 978-1-947627-33-8 (pbk. : alk. paper) |ISBN 978-1-947627-34-5 (eBook)
Classification: LCC PS3570.R5876 A6 2019 | DDC 813/.54—dc23
LC record available at https://lccn.loc.gov/2019009976

Cover and book design by Antonio Castro H.
Making his way in the international world these days.

FOR RODOLFO TRONCOSO G. & BERTHA E. TRONCOSO

FOR DOLORES M. RIVERO & JOSÉ L. RIVERO

TABLE OF CONTENTS

"What, then, is truth? A mobile army of metaphors, metonyms, and anthropomorphisms—in short, a sum of human relations which have been enhanced, transposed, and embellished poetically and rhetorically, and which after long use seem firm, canonical, and obligatory to a people: truths are illusions about which one has forgotten that this is what they are; metaphors which are worn out and without sensuous power; coins which have lost their pictures and now matter only as metal, no longer as coins."

—FRIEDRICH NIETZSCHE, *On Truth and Lie in an Extra-Moral Sense*

"All you need now is to stand at the window and let your rhythmical sense open and shut, open and shut, boldly and freely, until one thing melts into another, until the taxis are dancing with the daffodils, until a whole has been made from all the separate fragments."

—VIRGINIA WOOLF, *Letter to a Young Poet*

ROSARY ON THE BORDER

I am glaring at a casket: can that be my father, that shrunken, wax-like face? These idiots wouldn't put just anyone's body in there, would they? His face is so gaunt, his slight smirk now a permanent smeared smile. Did he lose that much weight? His mouth tight around his lips somehow, as if his skin is already stretching against his skeleton and melding with oblivion. Did they sew his mouth shut? When a body is embalmed, is it hollowed out and left as a meaningless sign for the living? When Ysleta's Mictlán Funeral Home—next to the Walmart on Americas Avenue—embalms you, well… But it's him, I think. It must be him. I haven't been home for a while, the rooms all seem smaller, my father…

Adán sidles up to me. He has lost a lot of weight, had his stomach stapled, but he looks shriveled somehow, not exactly healthy. I ask him, Is that our father? He reassures me. "Yes, of course, that's our father. He lost a lot of weight the past two months. Hey, can you read this tomorrow, at the mass?"

"Yes, okay." I know he knows I don't believe in these rituals anymore, yet he still trusts me. Or pretends to trust me. The dutiful, once-fat Adán, the priest-who-never-became-a-priest. He hands me a sheet inside a wrinkled plastic cover as my eyes trace the contours of my father's body. Maybe Adán just doesn't want me to screw anything up.

"It's easy. Take it. You'll sit next to me and Pablo tomorrow, and we'll be reading from the Bible too. I'll tell you when and everything."

Adán must've seen the nervous look in my eyes: I don't want to screw anything up either. For years, my older brother has volunteered at Our Lady of Mount Carmel. Me? I often imagined Christ-on-the-Cross rapt, and not from pain. Okay, I'm a non-believer, but I don't have to be an asshole about it.

In the middle of leaf-peeping season, I flew from Boston to El Paso for the funeral. Our father made it to eighty-two. That's something, isn't it? But I haven't been back since Christmas, when for six days I could only endure a few minutes alone with my father.

Mom's next to me. She kissed him a few minutes ago, when the family was allowed first dibs. A slow kiss on the forehead. Like she meant it, and she probably did. What's it like to kiss a dead man? Could pieces of his skin flake off on your lips? Here in Ysleta they did love each other for sixty years. Despite the arguments, our poverty. Despite the last two years of bedsores, and the diabetes killing Dad. Despite the urine-stink engulfing his bedroom and escaping into the hallway like a gas leak. Despite my mother fainting with fatigue, and my father holding her to "her obligations." Despite Mom, 'Señora Big,' too timid to fight back. She's always been too timid, and my father too lucky to find her in Juárez. As my father's body collapsed around him, my mother did not break, but Dad almost yanked her into the coffin with him to *el otro lado*. His mind never abandoned him, but diabetes destroyed his legs, his arms, his eyes, until he couldn't roll over in bed.

What was left was this demanding, bitter voice from the room next to the kitchen. Mom never stopped obeying that voice.

My sister is here with her daughters, three dark angels. Sometimes I like my sister Linda, and sometimes I hate her. I mean, she's old like me, already in her late fifties. She's disorganized, wasteful with money, still "taking classes." That hasn't changed since her twenties. Is this an unending school fetish? But you know, my father died three days after she returned from Virginia to Ysleta. Dad waited until Linda was next to him, his favorite, before buying front row seats for that big mariachi concert by Pedro Infante in the sky.

Her daughters are really good at praying. Undulating, like those Jews at the Wailing Wall. That's what I think a rosary service should be, even if I don't believe in it. At least respecting what Apá achieved in his life, the good in those green eyes despite their meanness. And I do respect it. Abandoning Mexico for the United States, which he kind of hated, to chase his girlfriend who wanted to be an American. Creating a successful life with less than nothing, while these whiny, red-faced Anglo clowns like Lou Dobbs poisoned the air we breathed. My father loved my mother in this desert for decades. If I think about it, he was a damn good father, there at home, even if he yelled at us, even if he once kicked the hell out of my teenage ass. Yesterday at the house, Elena Martinez, my sister's best friend from high school, whispered to me, "At least you guys had a real father. Ours was always drunk and gone." In Ysleta, that's a compliment.

More people coming in, sitting down. The neighborhood. What's that noise? Underneath the casket: a little metal cube whirring, emitting a fruity scent around us. *Capirotada* and mangos to mask the formaldehyde? But that body is not him anymore. That's not the man who worked two jobs, who wouldn't accept food stamps even if we qualified for them, who worked his sons worse than wetbacks. I always figured that's how Stalin did it, to take a country from nothing to something, through industrialization and into the Second World, with slave labor and no-excuses pain. That was my father. A crazed Mexican Vulcan, forging the meat of labor into capital. From nothing but dirt, to money in the bank. From a patch of desert a short walk from the *mordidas* of Narcolandia, to retiring at fifty-three and traveling to Europe with my mother, to Israel, to Egypt. My father was our Stalin-Moses: he led us through the desert into our forced industrialization, the good ol' American Dream. Maybe there was no other way. And that's a good Mexican family. I sure did learn how to sweat, how to bleed, how to fight back in Ysleta.

Tin-tan is here, that son of a bitch, Pablo's jester from the 'hood. One of the first ones, too. After all his jealousies because he had a shitty family and made stupid choices. So everything I did, my obsessions with Hinton in high school and Faulkner and Márquez in college, my leap to Boston, my making it as a prof from this desert nada, all of it because my father was "educated," and his wasn't? Dad went to agronomy school, for god's sake! Never saw him pick up a book in his life. And Tin-tan always with his fake smile reminding me on San Lorenzo Avenue that he had dug as many outhouses as I did. Who the hell cares! Does that explain why he's still a substitute teacher? Why is it that people who never left the 'hood get pissed off when you fail and succeed, and you fail again, and finally succeed, when your success somehow makes them look bad? Humans are a selfish, petty race. Look at that asshole, kneeling in front of Dad's casket, praying. Pray to climb out of your conceit, Tin-tan, pray for no more excuses before it's too late. Your horse-face and pissy attitude won't ever help you, bro.

God, here comes more of 'em. Cousin Adriana and her husband, Julio, the narco, ex-Mexican military. Her sister Alma, the whole crowd from Chihuahua. Loudmouths. Hugging everybody. It's not a coffee klatch! Rita, and the 'rich' California cousins. I think she's at least a university administrator near LA, but look at those Kimmy-K-tight dresses and faux cowboy boots, and yelps of joy with Adriana! I mean, there's a casket behind you. Dad the dead guy is waiting for a little respect. What's wrong with them? What's wrong with us? Sorry, Dad, for our family.

"*Sonríe!*" I hear a micro-second before two clammy hands squeeze my cheeks, and Adriana's maroon lips and raccoon eyes float in my face like a possessed Jack-in-the-Box. What the hell is wrong with my Mexican cousin? "*Por qué tan serio*, David? *Sonríe, hombre.*" Oh, my god, she's grabbing my face again! I want to punch her. I mean, is she mentally ill? This is a goddamn rosary, my father's dead, and she's telling me to lighten up? I step back from her, horrified, and she continues as if nothing's happened, to my mother next to me, to my sister, to her daughters, holding out her hand and wishing *them* condolences.

I glare at Adriana as she moves down the line. Her sister Alma is not like that, but Adriana, there's something seriously wrong with her. She's so self-absorbed, like her own dead father, my uncle, my father's brother. *El gran macho* from Chihuahua always visiting us in Ysleta, and bragging about his rancho, and piling it on in front of his little brother.

Making light of anything my father accomplished, the tight fit inside the living room of our adobe house, the interminable hours at Dad's construction jobs, El Paso and its dust storms, Ysleta and el barrio Barraca, the weed-infested irrigation canal behind our house. And what did my father say when Uncle Dago guffawed about his great rancho in Chihuahua, and how much *plata* he was hauling in with his government contracts and connections, and what bull he had castrated, all of it as Dago fucked bitch after bitch on both sides of the border? Aunt Esmeralda, *preciosa* like a matron from old Andalusia, full of pride back in Chihuahua? How exactly did my father ever respond? My father so timid, always deferring to his braggart older *carnal*. You know, that's why so many women have been slaughtered in Juárez. That's exactly why. This goddamn immortal machismo. This human corruption like *la leche*. This reduction of human relationships to those who can abuse and those who can be abused. You have to fight the fuck back, if you can. It's not about reason over there: it's about *movidas* and the hunger and cowardice of men, all in a sick Machiavellian fiesta. *Ajúúa!*

And Adriana, her father's daughter. So into herself, with her bawdy jokes, even when no one laughs. So willing to humiliate others. I mean, what twist of nature is it when the female of the species becomes the macho? I must have been mentally ill when I had a thing for her in high school. Adriana absorbed her father's personality, and spits on others with her "humor." Like an actress, at the center of every conversation. Only Julio she respects, her quiet psychopath sidekick so willing to let her be the show. Man, I almost punched her. "Smile! Why aren't you smiling at your dad's funeral?" La Donald-Trump-Mexicana. But I would not cause a fuss, not with my father's body a few feet away.

What is wrong with her? Like she's missing the neural net for respect. And maybe I'm too much my father's son. Maybe I'm just another grandiloquent smile in this wasteland desert. Another sheepish Mexican. If I had any guts, I would have shoved her face away.

What is she doing? Julio and Adriana in front of my father's casket. But reaching into the casket! Rearranging my father's hands! A flower? She's plucked a red carnation from the arrangement on the casket and shoved it into my father's hands! Who the—? What's wrong with her? Some nerve! Who messes with the dead body at a rosary? I ought to just yank her hair back. Goddamn Adriana. Her little brown eyes and pale face. It's a violation of my father. Jesus, I hate her. She's staring at my father, with her self-satisfied Minnie-Mouse look. My father, even in death, just another toy for her.

What's she doing now? Oh, my god! There she goes again! Anybody else seeing this? Who's protecting my father? Adriana's hands in the casket again, she with a slip of paper in her hand, arranging it. In my father's suit? What the hell? She steps back. Julio too. What have they done? I know Adriana's brother, *el pinche* self-satisfied Santiago, is an evangelical Christian, and has for years tried to convert my Catholic father and mother. I think Adriana and her brother are *Testigos de Jehovah*, or something like that. They're the loonies in suits roaming Ysleta my mother sics our German shepherds on. What did Adriana put inside the casket? That paper? That red-carnation kitschy atrocity. It can't stay there. It won't.

Decades ago, when I graduated from college—in fact, the only time Mom and Dad ever visited Boston—we were at South Station, the three of us sitting on a long wooden bench. I remember it was smoky—or at least dust hung in the sun's rays through the air. We were having a fight—or at least I was fighting with them. Commencement had been the day before, and I had accompanied them to Amtrak, because they were on their way to D.C. to make this trip a kind of vacation. Smiling in his smirky way, my father had quizzed me about what I would do now with a college degree in poli sci, when I would start work. He bragged about how he had survived alone in Juárez, after my *culo* grandfather had slapped twenty dollars into his palm and sent him out the door. I think my father always believed I was kind of soft, too emotional, not his kind of son, not the Mexican macho he adored in Uncle Dago, not the servant he saw in my brother Adán, not the athlete he admired in Pablo.

I was this strange creature who would and would not do what he wanted, who questioned his values to his face, who had created opportunities he only dreamed about, who had finished an American college degree in an American city as strange as Moscow would have been to any of us.

As we sat on that wooden bench and waited for their train, my mother defended my ambiguity, defended my wanting to keep searching for what I truly wanted, which of course, like any smart-ass twenty-one-year-old, I could not articulate very well. This college, this city had opened my eyes beyond Ysleta, beyond El Paso, beyond the border desert, and now just working to pay bills seemed like a prison to me. I knew I would not be able to think, and that's what I had relished in college for the first time in my life. A certain openness to my life that I did not want to close. His life had been defined by what he *had* to do; mine would be, I hoped, by what I *could* do. In his life, he fantasized about becoming a doctor and forever blamed his father for giving him nothing to achieve that goal. In my life, I had taken a rash leap away from home, made my way with little interference from my parents, and would not give up on my nascent dream.

My father criticized my indecisiveness, my wasting time at school without having a plan. It was more than just that he didn't want to pay the bills. And really, he hadn't paid the bills. I had worked every summer, work-study every academic year, I had taken shitloads of student loans, and yes Mom and Dad had sent me hundreds of dollars here and there. But I had carried the load to what I think he saw as a wild gambit in Boston, to this strange, faraway New England school without Mexicans. At graduation, my parents had been the foreigners, much darker than everybody else, with awkward accents, intimidated next to my roommates, friends, and their casually suburban parents.

It wasn't the money. It was another of my weaknesses, that's what he used against me at South Station. His green eyes glinted like the edges of Damascus steel. A snide little comment that sliced between my ribs like a switchblade, about my girlfriend, Jean, a blue-eyed beauty from Concord, Massachusetts. My lovely and loving Jean who had sought them out with her college Spanish, and laughed heads-together with my mother; Jean who had accompanied me to El Paso for Thanksgiving my senior year; Jean who was more delicate and sophisticated than the richest Anglo girl they had ever come across in El Paso, Texas.

My father at South Station: "Why would Jean want to stay with someone who doesn't know what he's doing? Who doesn't have a job? It's time to stop living in a fantasy world. It's time to be a man."

I hated him for pitting what he imagined Jean was and what he believed I would never be. I hated him for not believing in me, I hated him for not giving me another chance, I hated him for wanting to slam the door shut on what I could be. I told my mother—because I knew it would hurt her—and I told my father too—because he was next to her—I told them I had always felt abandoned and adopted, that they had always favored my brothers and my sister, that I knew I wasn't loved by them in Ysleta. I was shouting at them, even as hot tears slashed across my cheeks. I didn't care that a few others turned to stare at us in that waiting-room cavern. I didn't care about the propriety or impropriety of what others thought of me, unlike my father. It was the moment when I had felt the most alone in my life, more than that first day as a freshman when I had stumbled with my old suitcases into the dingy, one-room cell, carrying two dozen *flautas* wrapped in foil from Ysleta.

Thoreau, too, had once been in dark exile in Hollis Hall. I was that iconoclast's Mexican brother.

Only a few minutes to go, and they would have to leave for their train. I wanted to punch my father. My mother in tears said, of course, she loved me. My father held back, embarrassed, watching both of us as if we were insane, he averting his green eyes from mine. Waiting for him to stand up, I stared through him, my chest heaving in spasms. My mother's hand reached to hold mine, to calm me. I believed—and did not believe—what I had said. I still wanted to punch him.

I had felt so alone for so many years. Part of it was what I had done by leaving home. Part, too, was having never felt at home in Ysleta.

Then my father, inhaling, finally meeting my eyes again, said, "We love you, David, but sometimes we didn't know what to do with you. You are not like any one of us."

I think my father said these words because he never wanted to see my mother in pain. I think he said them because he didn't want to see his grown son angry and out of control at South Station, surrounded by strangers. He may have even meant what he said, too. I don't know.

We said our goodbyes. I hugged and kissed both of them politely. My head throbbed. I was alone, and I had always been alone, and they had been together and would always be together. It took me years to understand what this meant.

I made many decisions, some awful and others brilliant, but I found ways to keep that openness in my soul that meant more to me than breathing. I told them over the years what I was doing, how I was trying what no one in my family had ever tried to do. When I was failing, I admitted that as well, and they listened politely. I also knew that's all they could do. One lonely night in Connecticut, I pulled myself from a window's ledge. No one else next to me. Another day I chose to do something someone like me should have never accomplished, and yet I did, and kept going. I learned to recognize when others, like Jean, were much better than me, because they had faith in my soul. I believed in very little, but I kept going until I would get tired or defeated, and then I would take time to discover another wall to throw myself at. I was, and I am, and I will be, a peculiar kind of immigrant's son. I got old, and that made everything better, including me.

The next day I arrive first at Mictlán Funeral Home, my McDonald's one-dollar coffee in hand. The funeral director, who looks like Freddy Fender, arrives after me and opens the door for the "last-respects family visitation," before the casket is sealed for burial. I know my brothers will soon be here. My sister is bringing my mother for one last look at her beloved. I imagine she will kiss my father one last time. I finish my coffee before stepping inside.

My mother was crying last night, in Ysleta, in front of her bedroom. I could tell in her eyes she was lost, waiting, waiting…for him who would never return. I closed the other bedroom door where my father had died, to prevent the scent of urine from escaping to the kitchen. I looked at my mother as we sat in the kitchen. She trembled as she walked, my eighty-year-old mother, a homemade green apron around her black dress. Her eyes were bloodshot and drifting. She got up to serve Adriana and Julio salad, and she hugged Alma and Rita and asked about their children, the kitchen full of family just as the funeral home had been jam-packed earlier for the rosary. Someone even bragged about how many had attended the service. Old friends. Cousins. Neighbors. Visitors from Chihuahua to Los Angeles. *Los compadres y las comadres*. Neighborhood hypocrites and hangers-on.

My mother mentioned to somebody about that odd empty space next to the Formica counter, where the case of water bottles was now, that's where her husband would sit for hours in his wheelchair, with his television tray. She grabbed a tray of food, offered it to someone, or remembered she was about to offer it to someone, her mind suspended between thoughts, neither here nor there. I could tell she didn't know what to do, to be a host or not to be, to continue, and how to continue.

Over time she would be better.

When there was a lull in the conversation among the eaters at the kitchen table, she said, "*Ahora tengo que valer por mi misma.*" *Now I have to believe in and fight for myself.*

What an odd thing to say, I thought. She was so old, she wasn't a child or young adult anymore. Shouldn't you be doing that your entire life? Shouldn't you be doing that when there was still time for you? Both my parents had possessed timid personalities, my father having been thrown out by his father, my mother having endured her often violent mother. Sometimes I imagined them as "old children," still fighting wars that had ended decades before, frightened children-adults who had discovered each other amid the rubble.

But together they had not been timid parents, together they had accomplished more than most in this poor neighborhood. Together they had found—what?—something stronger than this godforsaken earth?

The funeral home's chapel is empty. I walk to the casket, and my father is there. Yes, it's him all right. Thinner, but it's him. I can't see his green eyes, but I know it's him. I'm alone with him for the first time in a long time. Strangely, I don't have any fear of death. That's one thing he has given to me. I look around at the empty pews. I am for sure alone with him. Is he self-contained? Maybe that's not exactly the right word. It's more like, what he is now is not who he was. That's over. What's left is this ceremony for us.

My father did what he wanted to do in his life. He married the love of his life, and he stayed with her despite their troubles and disasters. He was often different, even antagonistic, to who I was and who I would become. There were many times when we didn't understand each other, when we couldn't. The times that shaped us were also poles apart. Now, together again, with this strange result: I don't have any fear of death, now that I see it in front of me, now that I see my father. I do not fear that only this fragile armor of meat surrounds this self. I think Shakespeare was wrong, at least for some of us. Yes, I think, for some the undiscovered country is not death but life.

The little metal cube still hums and emits an orange scent underneath my father's casket. I take the stupid red carnation out of his hands. They are surprisingly stiff. I put the flower back inside the arrangement on the half-closed casket. I leave the rosary beads wrapped around his fingers because that's how he and my mother would have wanted him in eternity. I search the nearest pocket in his blue suit, and find Adriana's slip of paper. It is indeed a goddamn Jehovah prayer. I crumple it into my own suit pocket. I step back. Before I settle into my stance to guard him, a sort of privilege I now think, I hear the double-doors open behind me. I think I hear Adán's voice, and others, but I don't turn around for them. I face only my father and who I am.

NEW ENGLANDER

David smashed the sledgehammer onto the logs from his woodpile. The logs fell like small torsos on the black asphalt of his driveway. Each blow split a log in half, or jammed the heavy black iron wedge deeper into the oak with a groaning crack. His body and mind seemed to sing as he worked. His hands trembled. Even in the autumn chill of early November, sweat dripped behind his ears and released little shivers up his neck. His heart thumped inside his chest. Mid-swing, David sometimes imagined a bobcat lunging at his throat or a black bear rearing on its hind legs behind him. The trunk of a dead maple not far from his backyard was deeply scratched by a bear. Those scratches were at least three years old. In the forest, he and Jean spotted the "bear maple" the first month after they bought the nine-acre property in Kent, Connecticut.

This was David's first house, thousands of miles from his birthplace in the American Southwest.

Two hours before, Jean had driven to the Costco in Danbury to get ready for Thanksgiving. The boys would be coming back from college, for the first time with their girlfriends. The plan was to go hiking at Mt. Tom's State Park. Fifty-five-year-old David liked to hike even steep climbs. He was in good shape for an old guy. He promised himself he would be a good sport and allow his sons to stay in their rooms with their girlfriends and give them privacy. Last week, he had bought new Bemis toilet seats at Home Depot and threw out the cheap soft vinyl ones at the Kent Transfer Station.

As he split more logs, David remembered and was astonished that he had been only a year older than his youngest son when he and Jean met junior year at Harvard. After a few dates, David was shocked when Jean so casually invited him to her room. That startling impression never left him: the easy relationship with her body, that hopeful smile she flashed at him, her big blue eyes asking but not asking. David was a poor Mexican-American kid with a Torquemada Mexican mother from Chihuahua and a father who embraced a mixture of socialism and Catholicism. David shuddered to think what his parents would have done to him if they had discovered him with a girl in his room at home in dusty Ysleta. For many years he felt weird and defective in the Northeast.

It was Jean who helped him believe in himself. It took years of Jean loving him — this still svelte and gracious woman — for David to abandon his self-hate. After graduate school, Jean pursuing him and knowing exactly what she wanted, they married in Massachusetts. When Jean was diagnosed with breast cancer, the children toddlers, they fought together to survive. David bestowed upon her the toughness she loved in him. She in turn gave him enough love to make him whole, despite his in-laws, who feared he would whisk Jean of Concord back to El Paso. But why would that thought ever cross his mind, to go backward in his life, instead of forward, to leave this forest that woke every sense in his body? Connecticut was where he belonged now.

A scholarship boy at Harvard, David leaped beyond his father's construction projects on the Mexican-American border to become a professor at Rutgers just outside of New York City. After decades in a co-op on Manhattan's Upper West Side, David and Jean leaped again, beyond the City, escaping to an early retirement in Kent, to gardening and chopping wood and occasionally visiting friends after a night at Lincoln Center. David Calderon, a North Face jacket over a flannel shirt, lugging the cut logs into his four-bedroom Colonial, was now a New Englander. An avid reader of Emerson as well as Borges. A weekend craftsman who could just as easily fumigate his basement as affix a bright new American flag to the frame above his forest green front door. David had traveled a long road to Kent. Still, there was so much to do, so many more books to read, and so many more days and nights with Jean.

David picked up the last load of logs from the driveway. Panting puffs of little clouds around his head, he half-stumbled into the garage to place the logs in the black metal firewood rack Jean had bought for him from L.L. Bean. As he bent down to pick up the metal wedge and sledgehammer, he noticed a lone figure walking up his long driveway, a small gravel road just less than a fifth of a mile off Route 341. That was a feature of this house David loved: it was hidden from the main road amidst the trees, and nestled deeply in a valley of hundreds of acres of gently sloping hills. But during heavy winter snowstorms, he did not like paying $80 each time his Brazilian landscaper plowed his driveway. And Jean did not like the occasional feeling of isolation.

In Kent, Jean's visits to the True Value Hardware store for milorganite, the Davis IGA for groceries, and the small town library—

all of this reminded her of growing up in Concord. A top-notch Belgium chocolatier at the town center turned this small New England town into a jewel.

David marched quickly into the garage to place the wedge on a work shelf and the sledgehammer in the corner where he kept his growing stockpile of tools, the chipper/shredder from his in-laws, a Husqvarna chainsaw, a new weed-wacker. He walked out to meet the stranger coming up the driveway, but the man was already waiting for him on the black asphalt in front of the garage.

"Get the fuck back in the garage," the stranger growled in a gravelly voice.

David's smile drained away. He focused on the short, unkempt red hair, the steely blue eyes, and the unshaven nubs on the man's face. He saw a powerful forearm, a tattoo, and a hand gripping a shiny black handgun pointed at David's chest. "Are you fuckin' stupid? Get the fuck in the garage, unless you want me to drop you right here."

"Just take whatever you want." *Get him out of here. Get him away from you.*

"Shut up and close the garage door. Now!"

The garage door sputtered closed with its electronic drone. Instead of a buffer between him and the animals, snow, wind, or sheets of rain, the shut door felt like a sealed tomb. David's heart drummed faster, not tired anymore, adrenalin coursing through his blood and muscles. Wild thoughts spun through his head. Should he lunge at this man and try to yank the gun away? This crazy looked like a hardened townie, wiry, stinking of cigarette smoke and alcohol, his jeans ripped at the knees, what his father would have admiringly called an *obrero*, a worker. He had a slight Scottish or Irish accent. He was someone you might see at a construction site with a stack of rebars on his shoulders, and certainly not someone with the slightest bit of bluff. Maybe it wasn't the best idea to try to overpower this man, at least not now.

"Get in the house and shut the door."

"Please just take whatever you want. I'll help you carry it. Take my wallet, it's in the kitchen."

"Sit down and shut the fuck up," the man said, as he yanked bills from David's wallet and stuffed them in his jeans. As David stared at the intruder, he thought the man looked like Cormac McCarthy, one of his favorite authors, who was also from El Paso, except this man was thinner, his face more angular, but with that same wide forehead, the arms thick and tanned and freckled, the torso muscular and lean. It was the body of a man who might routinely go hungry for a day or two. David had once been like that at Ysleta High School, more lanky than chubby, but years of college and graduate school and working as a professor had softened David and left him with a slight paunch, an easy smile on his face, and the touch of gray at his temples—the looks of a distinguished older man.

The intruder stared out the window to the backyard, stepped to one side of the kitchen, and glanced out the front window of the cranberry red dining room.

"Please, just leave me alone. My name is David, and I live alone here. Please, take whatever you want." David thought about how victims should become people to their tormentors, not abstractions. He remembered he had read that in the "Week in Review" section of the Sunday *New York Times*. He thought: *instead of becoming a thing, become a someone*. David needed to keep talking to this man.

"Oh yeah, fuckin' David, so who the fuck is that on the mantel, your girlfriend?" the man said icily, glancing out the dining room window again. "No car, so whaddya do, walk the four fuckin' miles for groceries into Kent? If you lie to me again, you asshole, I'll put a bullet through your skull." Through the open window above the kitchen sink, David heard a siren approaching from the west on 341, a rarity on these country roads. In a few seconds the siren faded and suddenly stopped in the direction of Warren, the next town to the east. A helicopter's earth-shaking roar reverberated overhead and faded toward Huckleberry Hill. Were state troopers already hunting for this man? The town of Kent was so small, it could afford only one resident trooper, but the Litchfield barracks were not far away. Why did this man keep checking the front windows?

"Please leave us alone. Take whatever you want." David thought about Jean. How long would she be gone? He could not allow Jean to walk into this danger. He didn't care what happened to him as long as Jean survived, as long as she was never hurt.

"What's in the back over there?"

"A creek that leads to Lake Waramaug, I think. Over that ridge is another pond. A small road's on the other side of the pond, and it leads to the lake."

"Get me a fuckin' jacket as good as what you have on. Gloves, boots like yours, a hat." At once David stopped staring at the black gun in the man's hand or at his rough-hewn, pockmarked face, and noticed that this man was not wearing a coat and that he had sneakers for shoes. David walked to their mudroom, with a corner of his eye always on the gun behind him, which seemed to float in the air with a life of its own. David handed the man a pair of new Timberland hiking boots he had recently bought at the Sun Dog in Kent, the shoe shop for the scraggly and smelly through-hikers who emerged from the Appalachian Trail alongside the Housatonic River. David slipped off his jacket and handed it to him as well. He thought about El Paso and his mother and father. He thought about his boys, Matthew and Henry. He thought about Jean Catherine. He loved her more than anything else in the world. Whatever happened today, Jean had already saved him. This moron could never take that away. David could not allow this man to hurt Jean.

"Hey, asshole, you're gonna need one too," the intruder said, cracking a crooked smile as he slipped his arms into David's North Face jacket and zipped it up. The man glanced again at the long gravel driveway. It was still empty.

"Please, mister, you don't need me. Just take whatever you want. I love my wife. I love my children. You don't need me. I don't know what trouble you're in. But—"

"Hey, fuckhead," the man sneered in David's face, jamming the gun into David's chest. For a moment David thought about grabbing it, trying to grab it, but he didn't. "You don't want a jacket, then step the fuck out, and let's take a walk." The man shoved David into the living room facing the backyard, kicked him in the ass toward the patio glass doors, and shoved him into the doors before David could slide them open. David's face slammed against the metal frame. His brow was bleeding. For a second he saw stars in front of him as he stumbled onto the wooden deck.

"Over there. We're headin' down there." The man waved his gun toward the little creek, where David had always imagined the bear roamed. The rocky ledges formed small caves with the half-exposed roots of gigantic maples and oaks. They slowly descended the rough stone stairs his Brazilian landscaper had created with a forklift upending the earth and shoving massive stones into the side of the slope toward the creek. Jean had admired the landscaper's ingenuity. They had originally just asked the landscaper to create an open path to the creek, but he had presented them with the handiwork of these stairs that seemed to have existed in the Litchfield forest for centuries. David took one last look at his house, at what he had worked so hard to achieve, at how he imagined his family would suffer inside that house, at how everything would change forever for his boys, once their father's body was discovered in the forest. A tear burned across David's face.

What did this man want from him? They marched alongside the creek, over and around dead logs and meandering channels of water, deeper into a primordial valley of nature's matter. Sun-bright yellow and cinnamon-colored leaves covered the uneven, muddy floor. Oaks and maples and birches hovered overhead in the spectacle of a New England fall, a fluttery, animate ceiling. Would this man kill him? David had never seen him before, but that didn't matter one way or the other now. This man, David imagined, breathing hard, was being chased by the police. He was running away. Was David a hostage to keep the police at bay? Should he refuse to go on? Why did this man need him? If he stopped, if David refused to take another step, he would die. But if they lost themselves deeper in the valley toward Lake Waramaug, away from the house, what would stop this lunatic from killing David anyway? What would stop him from eliminating the only witness to his escape?

"Hey, keep movin'!"

"I'm not going anywhere. You don't need me. Please leave me alone. You're free. Just leave me alone."

"Did I tell you to stop? You fuckin' disobeying me, asshole spic?" the man shouted at David's face, shoving the gun barrel into his chest again. "Think I can't guess what the fuck you are? Dominican, Puerto Rican piece-of-shit." David imagined he was quick enough to snatch the gun from the man's hand, quick enough to grab the hand with the gun in it and give himself a chance. But the moment came and went, and the man stepped back, grinning, raised the gun, and pointed it at David's head. "Start movin' or I'm putting a bullet in your skull."

"No, please leave me alone. You're free. Please just go. I haven't done anything to you. I don't know who you are. You can go in any direction from here. I won't be able to tell anybody where you went. There's five hundred acres of forest all around us." A sudden revelation flashed through David's mind: *if this man shoots me, they will hear him.*

Suddenly, something hard—the barrel or the handle of the gun, David did not quite see what—smashed into his face. A piercing, blinding pain erupted in his head. Blood gushed into his ear, across one eye, and he raised his hands instinctively to protect himself. Another blow came from the other side, with a savage kick to his stomach. David collapsed next to the creek. He clenched his fists, and a horrible, wild anger seized him even as another punch landed against his neck and more blows rained on his head. Stunned and half-blinded, David instinctually grabbed a hand—it didn't have the gun—

and he wrestled with the man who still smashed the black gun barrel repeatedly onto David's head and shoulders. David was on his knees, and the man struggled to break free of David's grip. At once David grabbed a thigh, and like a savage bull, shoved his head and shoulders into the man's stomach. David and the man crashed on top of a pile of leaves hiding an upended tree stump. The man unleashed a guttural scream. David stumbled on top of him and lunged for the hand with the gun. Blood dripped from his face. For a second, he glimpsed the blue flames of the man's eyes, blinking, as splashes of David's blood fell on the man's cheeks. David gripped the gun with all his power, pushing the barrel away from him. He would die if he let go of the gun.

The man kneed David's back from behind, shoving his face with one hand. David struggled to stay on top of him and gripped the hand with the gun so tightly his knuckles whitened. He fended off the man's punches and grabbed the man's neck with his free hand. The gun exploded. The bullet missed both of them. They rolled on the ground, trying to grab control of the gun. With both hands, David finally pried the man's fingers off the gun. His back felt as if a vat of acid had been poured on it. The knees against his spine were like hammer blows. A flash of white light blinded him. Like a rabid animal, David bit the man's fingers, bit into the forearm with the tattoo—the man shrieked—and David yanked away the gun and flung it into the creek. The man twisted his head to find where the gun had landed, but he looked the wrong way and had not seen the gun sink into the creek's mud. David punched the man's face, punched until his fists and wrists cracked with pain, punched blindly as he felt the man's fingernails ripping the skin off his cheeks. The man's legs still kicked David's back, but weakly; he struggled underneath David's weight. David pinned him with his knees and thighs. He grabbed a log and smashed it onto the man's forehead, raised it and brought it down again, like a giant rolling pin, onto the man's face until the man's legs stopped kicking, until the man's hands dropped listlessly to the ground, away from David's face. Until the man was just a pulpy red mess of blood, eyes, and teeth.

David, gasping for air, collapsed next to his attacker. Blood was smeared on the dead leaves on the ground; blood covered the North Face jacket the man was wearing. David's yellow Oxford shirt was soaked in blood. Gurgling noises emanated from the man's broken nose. Little bubbles of white spume ran down his cheeks. Rivulets of blood dripped from David's head, onto his neck, into his ears, and for a moment he imagined it was raining blood. His face stung as if it had been whipped.

He stood up shakily. The man was still motionless on the ground. Bubbles had stopped popping from the man's nose. The man's chest stopped heaving in spasms. David tried to step away, but half-stumbled into the creek and its mossy and slippery banks. Where did the creek begin and where lay solid ground?

David's knee collapsed under his weight, and he could not move it. Maybe it was broken. He couldn't straighten out his back either, and he rolled onto the leaves again. The man was a few feet away, motionless. David didn't want to faint there, in the middle of nowhere. He closed his eyes and clenched his fists and stood up again, the rage in his brain burning through his pain, snapping his teeth onto nothing but air. Suddenly the world darkened for a few seconds. David wondered if had heard a noise behind him, a rustling in the leaves, a grunt. He imagined a bear, that bear, about to eat him. But nothing happened as he waited on one knee like a statue, for what seemed hours, waited for that black snout to puncture the skin on his neck or yank off the meat on his thigh, waited for the man to get up, like a lunatic Lazarus, and attack him again. For a moment, as David stared at the panoply of leaves again, away from the blood, he thought of Treebeard of Entwood from *Lord of the Rings*, his favorite book as a teenager. David imagined a giant branch-hand scooping him up and carrying him back home. He imagined the shadowy solitude of Thoreau's cabin. He imagined a black snout, his snout, clashing teeth against other teeth and ripping into a fleshy tongue. But in the next second, the blackness of the forest engulfed him. David passed out and fell face-first onto the muddy ground.

After a few minutes, David woke up with a harsh stinging in his left eye, and again turned his head toward his attacker. The man was not moving. Indeed, a few leaves had settled onto the man's chest and legs, his body already being claimed by the Litchfield forest. David lifted his shoulders off the ground, with wrists that stung with needle pricks of pain. An unbelievable agony, as if a branding iron had been thrust into his lower back, raced through his body. He could not stand up. After a few more tries in which he succeeded in lifting his torso only a few inches higher than the first time, David noticed his right leg was numb. Was his back broken too? Would he die next to this creek, one hundred feet from his house? David was crippled from the waist down. He raised himself off the ground. Hs arms, although stronger after three years of chopping wood, trembled after a few minutes of exertion. He dragged himself through the forest.

As he slowly inched away from the man and the mass of bloody leaves, David noticed how the world had shrunk to the few feet around him. To the leaves against his back as he hauled himself over the wet earth. To the branches he shoved aside, or the rocks too heavy to roll or lift away from his path along the creek. Water and mud crept into his pants, what was left of his pants. A warm, persistent trickle of blood dripped from the back of his right ear, as if the creek next to him existed also on his head. Certain jerks and shoves of his arms and torso, and an occasional kick from his semi-good leg underneath him, did not elicit the gasp-inducing hurt that shocked his heart. Only when he became impatient, when he attempted to drag himself more than a few inches at a time, or when his head, mistakenly, convinced him he could stand again and stop this torturous micro-movement, did he hurt himself so awfully he had to lie flat on the mud, close his eyes, and recapture his breathing before it fluttered away. *Eres muy terco*, David heard in his head, his Mexican mother's admonishing, yet admiring voice. *Eres demasiado terco, niño*. You are an unbelievably stubborn child.

David dragged himself along the creek. Occasionally he would hear his mother in his head, but more frequently David would hear his dead father. David remembered his father's stories about being thrown out of the house in Mexico, at eighteen years of age, with a handshake and only twenty dollars because his grandfather had wanted to make a man out of his son. David's father had often recounted these stories after he sneered at David for his weaknesses as a boy, for loving books and wanting to go to college in the Northeast and expecting financial help, for complaining about working construction for his father for no pay. David remembered how bitterly angry he had felt toward his father, even though his father had often acquiesced to pleas from David's mother not to turn every Calderon into an *obrero*. His father, too, had always mailed David checks to help him in college, despite the complaints.

Even if David had not been angry at his father anymore, he had also never forgiven him. For making him feel guilty. For the insults, obvious and imagined. For not ever openly congratulating David on how much he had achieved. Before David's father died, the father and son had hardly spoken to each other beyond the perfunctory "hellos" and "goodbyes" of an Ysleta Christmas, when David and Jean Catherine returned to his boyhood home in El Paso.

David could see, just around a heavy outcropping of black slate and tree roots, a glimpse of the Brazilian's stone stairs that led up to the backyard of his house. He pushed and pulled his body with all his might, imagined he had moved significantly, but then realized he had traveled perhaps a few feet in fifteen minutes. David's head was also woozy. White flashes erupted in front of his face. He blacked out again, only to find himself face-up, staring at the trees, a yellow leaf wafting toward his eyes. His numb leg, he noticed, had ballooned inside his pants. The thumping in his heart seemed to have picked up permanent speed.

David hallucinated about chickens, about carrying them in New England, two crazed chickens in each hand. This was the first job on a rancho near the Rio Grande his parents bestowed upon him as a twelve-year-old. Chickens stabbing at his thighs, chickens shitting in mid-air and on his sneakers, chickens pecking his eyes out, chickens

disemboweling him, hungry for his liver, digging for his kidneys…
David imagined swinging a sledgehammer again and again to obliterate
another wall, trapped in a gigantic maze of his father's walls, carrying
cinderblock after cinderblock until he dropped to his knees—glimpses
of his father shaking his head at him and David the teenager with a
murderous rage against all the blackness in front of him—working,
working, working beyond exhaustion. *Eres demasiado terco.*

As David dragged himself through the forest underbrush, his
mind incanted what seemed like a prayer. *My father. My sons. Can't give
up. Will not. God, please help me. Jean Catherine, find me. My father. My sons.
Can't give up, goddamnit. Help me, please. Fight. Will not pass out. Another
foot. Keep going, one more. Up these stairs, el gran Pelé at Maracaña. Fight.
Dear God. Goddamn Pilgrims. Fuckin' Aztecs. This earth will not defeat me.*

His body half on the first two stone steps to his yard, David
vomited onto his bloody shirt and over the stone step scraping his
elbow. A blinding white light of pain obliterated his mind. His swollen
right leg was twisted in front of him, a useless husk. He passed out for
a moment again, in a heavy sweat. When he opened his eyes, David
thought he heard another rustle in the brush below him, near the ferns
and hostas around the creek. *Can't give up. Keep going. Fuck. Goddamnit,
just keep going.* David dragged himself up another step and then
another, his body now draped on the final stone step. He was panting.
Leaves swayed above him. He could see the sun and had the sensation
he was underwater. He had pissed in his pants, and blood covered
his legs and shirt and face. He imagined the wild thumping inside his
chest could only go for so long before his heart exploded into pieces
as he lay half on the grass of his backyard and half on the sharp corner

of that final step, imagining a sea red with blood, imagining he was like a sculpture sinking to a bottomless pit beyond the sun above him. The trees. He could still see a few yellowish green leaves swaying in the wind. In the wind, a droning. The garage's door. *Can't give up. Keep going. My father. My sons. Jean Catherine…*

A LIVING MUSEUM OF LOVE

Before Sarah or anyone else downstairs came up to Stanley's bathroom, Carlos took the Cialis and jammed it in his pocket. No one would miss one bottle in a cabinet with maybe fifteen different prescriptions sitting beside them. Did Carlos have any clue what they're for? No. He studied revolutionary movements in Mexico, not pharmaceuticals. Stanley's daughters—Carlos's wife Sarah and his sister-in-law Deborah—would soon throw away the lot, and Carlos didn't care about the cufflinks, watches, and shotguns Deborah's husband Sam coveted from his dead father-in-law. *Okay, here I am, the Mexican stealing from my father-in-law. How crass is that? But Stan won't need these anymore.* Carlos alternately stared in the mirror and then turned to study the pills still left in the bottle he'd just stolen. Would he dare take one to see what would happen? He had already slipped two of the best old *Playboys* from Stanley's musty stacks in the attic: Jenny McCarthy, October 1993, and Stephanie Seymour, March 1991.

Three months ago, Stanley had died of a heart attack, and their house on the Merrimack River in Newburyport, Massachusetts would be up for sale in six weeks. Carlos thought about this grand old house, or at least how grand it had once seemed to him as a Harvard undergraduate from El Paso, Texas. Three decades ago. When he still wore more t-shirts and blue jeans than button-down Oxfords and khakis. When Sarah was this wicked-smart Jewish girl from the suburbs of Boston who loved canoeing and spoke Spanish perfectly, one of the many attributes Carlos's father and mother would come to adore about her. Three decades ago. Before graduate school, their children Jonathan and Ethan, and New York's Upper Westside. Before the "You-are-not-a-Jew" tomahawk to his chest by his future mother-in-law, Nancy, at the announcement of their betrothal. Nancy, Stanley's wife from Waban. Nancy, who had too often blurted put-downs from her cushioned throne in her kitchen like a rugelach bursting with nuts and raisins. Nancy who now, with slight dementia, sat helplessly, her face lost in the flow of the river, and smiled distractedly at her daughters and son and even her Mexican-American son-in-law. Carlos even loved his mother-in-law, despite the memory of her old attacks against "the Spaniard" her daughter was marrying. Was it the dementia or simply time and Carlos's stubbornness that had worn away his mother-in-law's hatred and pettiness? Was it his good relationship with his father-in-law, the erudite oncologist and once-Conservative Jew from Manhattan, who appreciated that his son-in-law had scored a tenured job at Columbia University, his old alma mater? Who knows what changes the human heart. Who knows if it changes at all. Maybe the objects around it simply change too, so the heart-in-the-world is only an older heart lost in a different world. The question then becomes: Are we the same person as our younger selves, or a collection of different selves in new worlds, or something disquietly suspended between the past and the present?

Carlos remembered the first week he had really met the

Mondsheins in Newburyport, when Sarah and he were writing their senior theses, she on the literature of revolution in Latin America — Mariano Azuela, José Vasconcelos, Martín Luis Guzman — and he on the Mexican Revolution itself, a historian-in-the-making. He remembered Nancy's "Spaniard" comment, which red-faced Sarah corrected in her offhanded way. Carlos also remembered making love to Sarah at the Mondscheins after a day of writing and work. In her old bedroom, while her parents slept downstairs, Sarah encouraging him, "As long as we keep quiet." She had jammed towels at the bottom of her bedroom door. The college boyfriend, Carlos couldn't believe her parents had allowed him to stay not just one night, but an entire *week*, to write their *magnum opuses* of their undergraduate years. He could only imagine his mother barging in with a cast-iron skillet to smash his head if ever he dared to bring a girl home and close his bedroom door in Ysleta. Or what his father would do, calling the father of the girl, the two joining together, with baseball bats, to teach these *sinvergüenzas* how to respect a Mexican home. Newburyport was like hitting the Mexican lottery for young Carlos: from the panoramic view of the Merrimack River in their living room with a black Steinway grand piano nobody played, to delicious Sarah every night, kind and sweet Sarah, Sarah whom he would marry years later. And now Newburyport, this house along the river, would be dismantled, sold, the Mondscheins but a memory. The patriarch was dead: Stanley Phillip Mondshein. He had indeed created different selves. Oncologist who had saved many lives and wouldn't stop lecturing his children about the country's healthcare problems. Intellectual who read David McCullough, Walter Isaacson, and *Playboy*. Jewish macho who was a revelation to his son-in-law from the United States-Mexico border. The Cialis jingled in Carlos's pocket as he walked into Sarah's old bedroom with its sunflowers-on-lime-green wallpaper and a human-size, stuffed green frog collapsed in one corner.

"Ready to go?" he asked a few minutes later as Sarah entered the room. She wasn't quite packed yet. They still had a long drive to New York City. Was she about to cry? Carlos jammed the Cialis deeper into a running sneaker. "What's wrong?"

"My dad…it's so sad."

Carlos hugged her. He had always loved her scent, which wasn't flowery or sweet, not like licorice or cinnamon, just Sarah's musky smell. He kissed her on the lips, kissed her big blue eyes which he never tired of studying. Oddly, they were her father's eyes. Sarah also had her mother's ample hips. In Carlos's mind, after three decades of being together, Sarah was still perfect, still the one he wanted, even if, if…well, she…said nothing, did nothing. This nothing in between them like a series of black walls nobody wanted to touch. Still love. But now with decades of nothingness to fill up the space in between…only walls he would occasionally make a half-hearted effort to breach…walls separating him from who he had once been on the border, for better or for worse. "Thank you for spending so much time here. You didn't have to. Just one more weekend, and we'll be done. Is that okay?"

"Of course. I'll be here. Where else am I going to be? You have any more boxes that need to go to the Dumpster? Anything else for the Highlander? I think we could get one or two more boxes in the back underneath your mother's wooden bench. There's still room."

"I got a text from Jonathan. He said he was going out with some friends tonight," she said, wrapping her arms around her husband. For years, Sarah had relished losing herself in him. Carlos missed these impromptu hugs so much.

"On a school night? Doesn't he have a term paper due this week?" Carlos pulled away, too tense to hold her anymore.

"Please don't yell at him. Please, Carlos. He's doing fine."

"Is that good enough for you? That's the reason Ethan doesn't drive, the reason Jonathan will be lucky to get into Fordham in three years. You don't push them. You cover for them. I was driving at thirteen—"

"'Cause your father needed someone else to haul cinderblocks, I know."

"Why are you interrupting me? Don't interrupt me. Am I wrong? Ethan should've gone twice to the driving school this weekend. What's his excuse this time? You let him off the hook. I would've forced him to practice with me if we were in New York. Saturday and Sunday. He's a smart kid, at least he's got that, but you don't learn to drive by thinking about it. You gotta get your ass behind the wheel."

"Carlos, please. Let's talk about it on the way home, okay. Deborah's choosing what Oriental rugs she wants, and what's left will be mine. Maybe one more box after that. Then we can go."

"Deborah's choosing 'her rugs'? I thought you were going to divide them. Even. Please, don't be a dupe."

"I got the china I wanted. Dad's paintings. You want anything else? Just shove it in the car. Please. Mom doesn't want much at Arbor Gardens. Whatever doesn't fit, we'll pick up next week."

"And your sister got the nicest pieces of furniture. The grandfather clock from Sweden. The Shaker table and chairs. Even the chipper-shredder and your father's antique motorcycle." Carlos had often disliked how his sister-in-law smiled to get her way, how she slyly turned conversations to her "brilliant" kids and her cocker spaniel, how she pretended to care about others. Sarah, Deborah, and even Sam were all black-belts in passive aggression. For three decades, Carlos thought himself an amateur taking lessons from pros. In Ysleta, he would've simply shoved one of his brothers in the chest if they had crossed him.

"Deborah's the one who found Arbor Gardens. She's arranged for all the painting to be done for Mom's rooms. Getting the furniture she wants moved there. She's been packing her all morning. We're almost done."

"Okay, fine. Deborah's done a lot. Your mom okay? I mean, all of you are going through her stuff, and she just sits there staring at the river. She doesn't have a choice, I know. But has she said anything to you? How's she feeling about all this commotion around her?"

"She's happy to have a nice place to go. I think she'll love Arbor Gardens."

"Your mom, when I talked to her, when I brought her coffee this morning, she apologized to me. She apologized for treating me badly. She told me I was a good husband." Carlos could see Sarah getting teary-eyed again.

"You see, she's not evil. She loves you, Carlos. So did my dad. He knew you had started from nothing, just like he did. He always admired that."

"I know, I know," Carlos said, his voice breaking just once. He did feel some sort of allegiance to Stanley. From the very first day in Newburyport, Carlos had never felt adequate about who he was, a poor kid from the border. Without support, without encouragement, he dared to choose the life of the mind, instead of becoming a lawyer, which he had thought about, which would have brought immediate recognition from his mother-in-law Nancy, his sister-in-law and her husband, and their friends. Carlos's father and mother thought their son was crazy: the life of the mind was not for a Chicano from El Paso. "Can you make a living as a historian?" his father had said in Ysleta years ago. "Are you out of your goddamn mind? You're turning down law school?" Sarah was the one who gave him the space and time to achieve his doctorate, Sarah was the one who had always earned more money than him, even after his tenure as a professor, and Sarah was the one most proud when his first and second books won accolades, despite that she had sacrificed her time with Ethan and Jonathan as children to become a partner in her law firm. For years, they had made their uncommon bond work, but Sarah had never forgiven Carlos for depriving her of the motherhood she had envisioned for herself. Ironically, only his father-in-law had truly understood Carlos. His Jewish 'other father' who had always wanted to write a book, but never had. The doctor-intellectual who never tired of arguing history and politics at the Newburyport kitchen table. Stanley Phillip Mondshein. Turn any name in the sun and one will always discover a new refraction of dark and light. "We'll come back as often as we have to. Make sure your mother's taken care of. That's what your father would have wanted."

"Thank you. It's not too much driving?"

"Five hundred miles each weekend. But it's fine. We need to do it. You need to be here with your mother. She didn't remember, by the way."

"Who didn't remember?" Sarah asked, already on her knees, packing her suitcase. Her sneakers, shoes, pants, a few family photographs for their New York apartment. Her head was but a few inches from Carlos's waist, and he remembered—how could he not?—how a young Sarah used to smile slyly at him for no reason, without warning, and just start to unbuckle his belt, and unzip his khakis… *What is wrong with me? What the hell is wrong with me?* Carlos thought.

"Your mother," Carlos said, sitting down on the bed and adjusting his pants. "She didn't remember what she said when we told her we were engaged. She didn't remember what she said at our wedding, in the kitchen downstairs. She didn't remember. But she was sorry."

"Well, that's how it is. Her memory comes and goes. I'm glad she said she was sorry. She probably remembers she said something bad. I know she does."

"I just brought her the coffee and she blurted it out. Even if she doesn't quite remember why, I'm still glad she said it. It meant a lot to me." Carlos forced himself not to get choked up. *Why does it still matter to me? Why am I still fighting battles decades old?*

"I love you," Sarah said.

After three more trips to the Dumpster in the driveway to dispose of what all of them did not want, their cars full, they were done. Perhaps one more visit to Massachusetts next weekend would finish the job of cleaning out Sarah and her sister's childhood home.

Carlos and Sarah drove for four hours, from Interstate 495

South to 90 West, the Mass Pike, to I-84, to Route 15, which after New Haven became the Merritt Parkway, to the Hutchinson River Parkway, joining the Cross County Parkway, finally to 9A South and Manhattan's Upper Westside. Carlos memorized the route like the lines on his face. Sarah never drove anymore. Sometimes he imagined he was a lighter-skinned Morgan Freeman, "Driving Ms. Sarah," without the hat. Carlos often made life convenient for his wife, dropping her off in front of their apartment, after which he drove three subway-stops away to dump the Highlander in their garage just west of Lincoln Center. She texted him they needed whole milk for tomorrow's coffee. Carlos walked home, not really wanting to get there quickly, unless he was more exhausted than he was. Tomorrow he would prepare for his classes and finish that research paper on Zapata in the stacks of Butler. At home Sarah would be talking to Jonathan or Ethan, if they were around, and getting dinner ready. He would be just like an invisible father-butler, in the way, trying to find a Yankees game on TV, feeling that distant look in Sarah's eyes every time she walked into their bedroom. *Why are we even together anymore? Why isn't she more affectionate? Why does she torture me like that? She got everything she wanted. And now she hates me? It's never enough. But why am I blaming her? Maybe there's a problem with me.*

Carlos hated himself for wasting time with these thoughts as he walked north on Broadway to stretch his legs. It was a gorgeous October day in Manhattan. He had forced her to work, when young Sarah would have been quite happy as a stay-at-home mom. That's what love did: it warped them into different selves. His schedule was much more flexible than hers, which she had never stopped resenting.

For her, weekends became sacrosanct time to be with Jonathan and Ethan. Carlos thought they should already have learned to be on their own and not be depending on their mother to remind them constantly about college applications, term papers, driving lessons. The Mondscheins were like that: always on top of their children, a family trait they had passed from generation to generation. Can anyone ever escape these cycles of history within a family? Carlos never forgot when he asked Sarah a question at the Newburyport kitchen table years ago, and her mother Nancy, without skipping a beat, answered for her daughter, as if Sarah had not been a New York lawyer but still a teenager in Massachusetts. That's how it often was in that family. His parents from Juárez loved him, but that meant they pushed him out of the house and encouraged him to take fifteen-mile bike-rides on weekends by himself—as a grade-schooler, through traffic, with only a "God be with you!" at his back. After Carlos had announced to his parents (who didn't speak much English) that he wanted to apply to colleges in Boston, and after he was accepted to a school he had never visited and in a state he knew nothing about, his father handed him three hundred dollars. "The rest is up to you, Carlos." The first and only time his parents visited him in college was when he graduated. It was brutal, but also clarifying.

"Excuse me," Carlos said to Sarah as he worked his way around her in the kitchen to put the milk in the refrigerator. He had waved at eighteen-year-old Ethan on the couch, engrossed in his computer. To interrupt him, Carlos walked over and kissed his son on the forehead. Sarah was chopping a tomato and mozzarella in slices. His younger son Jonathan was nowhere in sight. Carlos had overheard their conversation about Ethan's "personal essay" for college. This past summer Carlos had driven Ethan and Sarah to a dozen colleges, from Maine to Pennsylvania and back.

"Dinner will be ready in about fifteen minutes."

"Okay, thank you. Ethan. *Ethan*—" Carlos said, as soon as his son looked up from the screen. "I'm happy to look at the essay too, when you're ready. I wrote about my abuelita and how much she had meant to me in El Paso. She had shot and—"

"—killed a man who attempted to rape her during the Revolution. I know. Great story. Thanks, Dad. I'm gonna have Mom look at my essay first, if that's okay."

"Of course." Carlos stared at Sarah for a moment. She hadn't looked up from her cutting board.

"I'll show it to you by the end of the week, okay?"

"Yes, of course. Whenever you want. I'll be ready."

Later that night, in the semi-darkness still made possible by the micro-blinds in their bedroom, when Sarah reached over perfunctorily to kiss him goodnight, Carlos noted the chill on her lips, noticed they only remained on his cheek a second (never an instant longer), noticed she never pressed her body insistently into his anymore to say, "You're not tired, are you? What if I…you know…get ready? I miss you." For months, and then a year, he had initiated their lovemaking until it occurred to him that she didn't want to make love anymore, that she did it because she had slept with him for decades, but not because she wanted to be with him. There was no great argument. No smashing doors closed. No walking out. No drama at all. Just a cold, friendly kiss that burned on his lips for many minutes after he could hear her softly snoring asleep. Wiping that kiss away in the darkness was always what allowed him to get some rest. *Does everybody reach a point in life when you're dying more than you're living?*

The fall was his favorite time in New York, breezy and cool, with that anticipation of the holidays at the end of the year, that excitement at the beginning of every academic year lingering in the air. At Columbia University, the young women still sunbathed next to the statue of Alma Mater on the steps. In front of Butler Library, a young man in a red t-shirt, with a goatee, leaped miraculously through the air and grabbed a Frisbee and slid on the grass, like an outfielder snagging a fly ball in shallow centerfield in a spectacular play for the Yankees. Carlos had never been that carefree as an undergraduate, never that fit or confident, but he liked seeing those young people. He loved teaching them Mexican history. He imagined them as selves of what he could have been, perhaps how his sons would be in college, without the abject poverty of the border like a boulder strapped to the back of their heads, without the fear of the self that does not belong, without that weakness that distrusts and dismisses its own voice. Sarah had helped him through all of that. He would always be loyal to Sarah in his heart because of her patience with him. If they could just break down these walls between them—after the kids left for college?—then maybe they could thrive again together, maybe they could recapture a new version of their relationship. Was it too late for another metamorphosis?

A student in his seminar on "Major Battles of the Mexican Revolution," had asked him a series of questions, which preoccupied his mind like fireflies flittering around a porch light.

Carlos flashed his ID to the guard at the library entrance. The guard grinned at him, he knew Carlos well, he recognized him, but Carlos could not help but be formal, a mask he donned to keep anyone from bothering him. Intimidation. It worked.

That inquisitive young woman in his seminar reminded him of Christina Sierra, a girl he had a crush on at Ysleta High School in El Paso. Chocolate brown hair. Black coal eyes. Her skin so clear and pallid that it seemed to shimmer.

Like his seminar student, Christina had also owned a slim and pretty figure. But that's not why Carlos had "loved" Christina, as much as a chubby, geeky high-school senior can pine for a friend without actually doing anything about it. Plenty of girls from Ysleta High were gorgeous, even voluptuous. Christina wasn't like that necessarily. Yet she was smart, she was eloquent. She gleefully argued with young Carlos, and he never intimidated her. That was her attraction: Christina Sierra was an aggressive, intelligent, pretty Chicana who was his equal. She wasn't like his mother, who obeyed his father out of instinct and fear. She wasn't like many of the other girls at Ysleta High who obsessed about hair and makeup and the stupidities of fashion, or flirted with the jocks, or ass-kissed the popular teachers, or pretended to be rich when no one in Ysleta was really rich. Christina was "modern," that's how teenage Carlos had phrased it to himself.

That's why he went away to college, to find more modern women and men, to become one. That's why he fell in love with Sarah, a confident college student, and why he still loved her. The young woman in his history seminar possessed that same magical mixture

Sarah had: nerve, beauty, intelligence, and youth. Always a remarkable whole.

Carlos thought about the exchange in class earlier that day, the past often the present in his mind.

"Professor Garcia, I understand how Villa's decisions before and during Celaya put him in such a precarious military position that he had to resort to desperate measures. But I have a more philosophical question. I don't know if we have a few minutes just to talk about it, before we end our class. But…well…why do we study history, really? Why does it matter to study history in general, and why this history in particular? About Villa, for example?"

"Well, Natalie, that's an important question to end our discussion with. I think the broad answer is that we study history to study how people and societies work, but even more importantly, how they change. History, in a way, is a laboratory of facts, what actually happened to determine our present, and these happenings are complex, with no easy answers, and a lot of missed opportunities. This particular history we are studying in a way *explains* Mexico and the government formed after 1917. For example, if Villa had appreciated Obregón's defensive postures at Celaya early, if El General had used his cavalry to outmaneuver Obregón, instead of the frontal attacks that so decimated the División del Norte…if Villa had used reserve forces to counteract Obregón's maneuvers during the second battle in April of 1915…or if Villa had retreated to engage Obregón at a more favorable spot, where the Constitutionalists would not be so defensively entrenched…the course of the Revolution would have been different. Would Villa have eventually defeated the Constitutionalists if he had avoided the disasters of Celaya? Maybe, maybe not. But if he had avoided Celaya by adapting to and learning from the modern warfare of Obregón, then Mexico could be very different today. Perhaps a country implementing more of the Revolution, rather than paying only lip-service to it." Carlos was in full lecture mode for a few seconds, as his over-subscribed seminar of twenty-two students listened attentively. He rarely turned away any junior or senior who wanted to take his seminar, and lately even his lecture course on Latin American social movements had been packed. The chairman of his department had just asked him if he wanted to be Director of Undergraduate Studies for the next three years.

"I understand what you're saying, professor. But Villa didn't adapt. Villa didn't learn from that first battle that maybe his original strategy to engage Obregón at every turn—even when Obregón chose the terrain—was wrong. There's a sense of fatalism, I think. That's how I look at history. We could argue that Villa could have been a different man. One that could adapt, and go against his troops, and go against the image of himself, to think outside his own box, so to speak. One that could react in the present in a way that would make him succeed in history. But he wasn't a different man. He didn't act differently."

"Do we have any evidence that Villa *could have* acted differently? Remember, Natalie, if we look at history as only 'it could never have happened differently,' what we are doing is undermining the power of human choice, reducing to nil the real possibilities at most historical turning points that could have led to radically different histories."

"Well, that letter you showed us, Professor Garcia, the one Villa sent to Obregón in between the first and second battle, to offer fighting anywhere else but Celaya to prevent civilian casualties. Which Obregón rejected. I mean, Villa *knew* he was in a bad position. To keep attacking in the same way just meant more slaughter, especially on his side. But Villa still did it the next day anyway: he marched into who he was, his destiny."

"You are right, Natalie. Villa didn't adapt enough at Celaya, although many historians, and I am one of them, believe he had the capacity to adapt and learn on the fly, so to speak. Go against his nature. He often used unconventional methods in warfare. But even as historians—and those who use history who are not historians—we are changed by what we learn from the past, from what happened to Villa. By studying history—to get back to your original and very important question of *why*—we not only learn how the Constitutionalists won, how Mexico was formed politically after the Revolution, but we also learn how we might act in similar situations today, how we might act to either further a revolution or another cause for justice, or how to avoid the messy and murderous aftermath. So we also study history to appreciate, in real time, what might happen today in similar circumstances. What we might do at critical moments of decision-making in the present."

"Thank you, Professor Garcia. That makes a lot of sense to me."

"I'll be having office hours on Wednesday and Friday, at my office in Butler in the afternoon, so sign up. I'm happy to talk to anyone and to keep these lively discussions going. Remember, your first paper of the semester is due next week. Email me if you have questions. I'm happy to answer them."

"Professor Garcia. I know we're out of time. And this is a silly question." Natalie blushed as the students, half out of their seats froze to look at her, some grimacing, others smiling—she was the one who always asked the most questions at every seminar. "You really saw Obregón's arm in Mexico City? In a jar?" Titters of laughter erupted inside the classroom. Nobody moved, and a few even sat down again.

"His right arm. He lost it two months after the Battle of Celaya in 1915, in another battle against the Villistas. A shell explosion. For decades, they kept the arm in a jar of formaldehyde under a monument at the Parque de la Bombilla in the San Ángel neighborhood. The same spot where Obregón was assassinated in 1928. The arm floated in this clear liquid, and you could see the sinews and veins under the light." More nervous laughter scattered through the back of the room.

"That's kinda gross and fascinating at the same time."

"That's Mexico, in more ways than one, a kind of living museum. The arm was finally cremated in 1989, and the ashes spread over his grave in Sonora. I personally think they should've just put the arm back with the body, to make it whole." As student rose to leave, he called, "See you next week."

As his students strolled into the hallway outside his classroom, Carlos relished overhearing the macabre discussions and mini-debates about what *they* would've done with Obregón's arm. His favorite comment: "Think about what we could do for Halloween! Just think about it! That'd be so lit."

The stacks of Butler were now deadly quiet, as memories of his day receded and the present, its musty book smell in particular, pressed into him. The door to his office was open, the space more like a glorified closet lined with bookshelves up to the ceiling, each shelf stacked with monographs, history reviews, old newspaper files, and books, dozens upon dozens of books.

It was almost ten p.m. by the time Carlos walked the thirty blocks down Broadway and finally reached their co-op. He had already texted Sarah that he would stay late working on the Zapata paper. He had lost himself in the stacks; his brain burned with a pleasant exhaustion. His legs were not tired, but he still felt he would have a chance at a good night's sleep if he walked home. When he opened the door, Jonathan and Ethan were either in their room—the door was closed—or out with friends. The light was on in the kitchen, and Sarah came out in shorts and a t-shirt, already comfortable for the night. Carlos dropped his book bag next to his bureau and kissed his wife, who had a worried look on her face. A problem at work? Jonathan again? Or some other disaster? He took off his shoes, grabbed a t-shirt and a pair of shorts from the top of the closet, and started undressing.

"Ethan went running today, with Zendon Wong. Remember him from the River School?" Sarah stood near the closet, in front of the bathroom as Carlos hung up his khakis and L.L. Bean button-down shirt.

"Guess so. Everything okay? The kids okay?" Carlos's bare feet felt alive as soon as he was out of his shoes, his skin breathing again, the heat and moistness from his long walk causing his skin to stick slightly to the hardwood floors. He remembered running *descalzo* through the unpaved streets of Ysleta.

"The kids are fine. They're working in their room, or listening to music. They're fine." After a long pause, Sarah continued, as soon as Carlos slipped on his t-shirt. "Ethan couldn't find his sneakers. I lent him yours."

"Okay, that's great," Carlos said quickly, about to step into the bathroom, but Sarah did not budge from the doorway. He looked at her eyes, waiting for her to move, and then at her hands, and he saw the bottle.

"What's this? What are you doing with my father's Cialis?"

"I…okay…I took it. I stole it when we were in Newburyport this weekend. You would have thrown it away. You did throw away everything else he had." *I haven't really done anything wrong. I was just trying to save something that might…*

"But why did you take it? Are you having an affair? What's going on?"

"No…no. Nothing like that. We haven't, you know, played in a long time. I thought it would help me do better. I thought somehow I could make you happier. I didn't know what I was going to do with it. I just took the pills and put them in my sneaker." *I love you, Sarah. It's been hard, but I love you.*

"You're not having an affair? Carlos, look at me."

Carlos stared at the blue eyes he had loved for decades. "No. I am not having an affair. I want to have an affair with you. I want to sleep with you. Can I close our bedroom door, please?" He continued: "When's the last time we slept together? You even remember?"

"That's not your fault. It's been too long, I know. But sometimes, I don't know, I'm tired, too much pressure at work. When we have those few moments on the weekend, sometimes I feel we're just…just… getting over another argument. I don't want to much anymore." Tears dribbled down her face. "I just don't, I'm sorry."

"Sarah, I love you. It's fine. We're fine. I'm sorry I took your dad's Cialis."

She smiled. "I never knew he was taking it. I guess he was taking it for his prostate. A lot of older men take it. A lot of older men also take it to relive their youth. Imagine my surprise when I found it in your sneaker." She half-snorted. "I love you too. Maybe I'm just old. Maybe that's it."

"I'm old too. We'll be old together, right?"

"But you still want to. I know you do. Carlos, you know you were never the problem. Not there. I…I…when I was with you. Most of the time. You were wonderful." Sarah slumped on the bed, and more tears dripped onto her shorts.

"I loved being inside you. I still do. When we stopped, I sometimes felt like I was dying a little every night. We were dying a little every night. Already history. I wanted to try something different. It was an impulse, a stab at trying something different. I'm sorry I took the Cialis." He sat next to her, holding her hand. Her eyes still staggered him.

"I'm old, I'm old, I'm old."

"Sarah, please. I love you. I'll always love you. I'm not going anywhere. It's okay."

She stood up, walked to her dresser, opened the bottle, and gulped down four pills with a glass of water. Her comely smile greeted the alarm on his face, his eyes widening like brown moons above New York City. "It's fine, it's fine. I read about it. These are low-dosage pills. Only 2.5 mg. Maybe my father was only taking one per day."

"You shouldn't be taking somebody else's medicine. You sure? What are the side effects? Can women take them?"

"Yes, of course. Especially older women. 10 mg is good for an 'immediate effect.' Not dangerous. I've been reading about it on the Internet. It's worth a try."

"Okay, then I'm in too." Carlos took the bottle from Sarah's hand and also swallowed four pills after he stared at the prescription for Stanley Phillip Mondschien. "You're sure we're not going to have a heart attack, a stroke?"

"Don't think so. I feel fine. Feel good. I'll make sure the door's locked."

"I'll turn off the lights and get new matches for our candle."

"A glimmer of—where are you? What if this doesn't work?"

"I love you. We're here now. At least we're both trying. Isn't that what matters?"

As Carlos kissed Sarah, he kept thinking of the Spanish slang word *arranquin*, to jump start, to leap into what one wants, to find by looking, to go where love was and could still be.

THIS NEW NOW

"Why did you get that disability insurance, Ben?" Galilea glanced at her iMac as she spoke to her husband at work. "We can't afford it. You see the dental bill?" She noticed the dusty grime on the desk phone. The phone she held felt suddenly slippery. Their cat Ocistar stretched out on the bed under the sun, his paws quivering with delight.

"I called NetLife. We met our yearly maximum."

"In one crown," she said. "In one crown! It's $7,000 we're responsible for. And it was elective. At least you could have done one in December and the other two in January. I'm sick to my stomach."

"Gali, please. I just…should have thought about it. We like 59th Street Dental. Maybe he was trying to rip me off. But he explained it."

"We don't know our own dental insurance, what it covers, what it doesn't. I mean, if you don't ask questions, these doctors rip you off. They do whatever they want. Maglione never charged that." Ocistar raised his head at her, admonishing her with his eyes for disturbing his sleep.

"Because Maglione didn't do anything, he just kept postponing my dental work. Kingsberg said it was this deferred, dental work I hadn't done, four crowns Maglione hadn't done."

"Seven thousand dollars. What are we going to do? My parents never spent anything on our crooked teeth, and we didn't go to any doctor until we were suffering. And I mean, severe, I'm-about-to-pass-out pain. We spent $10,000 each on Livia and Emma and their braces! My god! Maybe I should start throwing money out the window, maybe I should buy myself jewelry for my nose!" Beyond the flat cat, Galilea could see the Hudson River through the window, an occasional barge or sailboat floating between the columns of buildings.

"Gali, please. I'll cancel the disability insurance. It was portable. No prior health check. That's why I got it. You know, it's been almost five years." Ben spoke with a catch in his throat. "That's the threshold. I got it in case—"

"Really? You want to cancel it? It is more expensive than everything else they're deducting from your paycheck. I just don't know how we're going to pay the $7,000. The kids' tuition bills are coming due in two months! I just, I just…"

"But look what happened to your father. Look at my mother now. One wrong step, and it's thousands of dollars down the drain taking care of her, home-health aids, rehab, doctor bills—"

"Maybe you shouldn't cancel it. It won't even be enough if you do. Where do we get the money for these crowns? Should we not pay the college tuitions? Which one? Both? Neither? I spend $175 on my teeth all year, for a teeth cleaning. That's it! That's what you get living with fluoride in Texas. Didn't get much else."

"I'll cancel it. That's $2,000 for the year. We don't need it. I'll be fine. Love you," Ben said gently over the phone.

"I'll take care of you if something happens to you. I'll take care of you. Still need to find $5,000 from somewhere else. I don't blame Kingsberg. It's our fault. Goddamn NetLife."

"Should've never switched from Maglione. But you liked 59th Street Dental. The kids liked him. Last year he did a great job on Emma's chipped tooth."

"You're blaming me for this?" Galilea said.

Ocistar stood up, arched his back, circled his spot on the bed, and curled himself into a ball, his tail wrapped around his hind legs.

"I'm not blaming anybody for anything. Have to get this call."

Galilea hung up the phone and sighed. Her husband worked at a small firm in Brooklyn where he was an architect and partner, which only meant that if the firm failed, he would fail too. It had been a rough three years. The country was in the grips of what some called a "new normal." Few appreciated exactly what it meant: the nation's greatness had been a fluke of geography, history, and wars, and middling existence would become an achy, intolerable demise. She didn't feel any better, venting, and her heart thrummed inside her chest.

She stood up, walked through a short hallway and into the living room, and turned into another bedroom. Galilea sat at the girls' old desk, surrounded by high school textbooks, a giant Harry Potter wizard's hat, four stacks of playing cards, three arrowheads, an empty bottle of Heublein's The Club "Manhattan" Cocktails, from an indefinite year, probably pre-World-War-II, with an amber hue and faded label, next to other historical junk Livia had purchased at antique stores and swap meets in upstate New York and Connecticut. Livia had abandoned the bric-a-brac in her room before leaving for college in Chicago. This desk was the one place where Galilea could design her websites for nonprofit organizations, political consultants, and small biotech companies without hearing too much of the pounding and door-slamming from the renovation across the hall, already a year in progress, the project of a hedge fund manager who was combining three one-bedroom apartments on what was a quiet floor. An Ivanka Trump look-alike was in charge, the new girlfriend, post ex-wife. Galilea pushed on her laptop. Sometimes she closed her eyes and imagined the dozens of paperbacks, empty antique soda bottles, Benzoline brass torch, crystals and pyrite, and model-UN award gavels from both her girls, all of it crashing onto her computer below, and smothering her alive.

The Upper Westside of Manhattan, as lively as it was on the surface, also hid underneath it the edges of a great river not far from the Atlantic Ocean, these edges eternally eroding into the watery depths, the crowded island fragmenting over time, a whole now, a part before, which was itself a whole one time, and a part before... At 97th Street and West End Avenue, next to the mighty Hudson River, bicycle and jogging paths of asphalt collapsed, a chunk of bedrock mica loosened and crumbled into the river.

Galilea stared at their ocicat Ocistar, who had pursued her to the second bedroom and stretched on a fleecy blanket on Emma's lower bunk behind the desk: his yearly vet appointment was coming up in a week, putting them another $400-plus in the hole, with cat vaccinations. *How much could I get for a twelve-year-old kitty? I'd have to pay someone to take our Preciosini.* Galilea scratched the cat's chin, as he playfully swatted her hand. *In San Elizario, we would've just let you run wild outside, until you were hit by a truck. Kids with crooked teeth? Well, don't smile too much. Seven thousand dollars for crowns? We talking about diamonds and rubies and all that crap?* Galilea fetched herself another cup of coffee to calm the acid sea sloshing inside her stomach. Ocistar followed her to the galley kitchen, rubbed her leg, pointed at his bowl with his face, and meowed. Why did they live in a cramped two-bedroom in Manhattan? How was it that she and Benjamin, in their mid-fifties—with their backaches and paunches and their gray hairs in weird recesses and sex life reduced to a pair of pecks once a day—could be here? In this wearisome now?

"So you're from San Eli! Wow. I miss their asaderos."

On Cinco de Mayo, a friend of a friend on Facebook had forwarded the message to Galilea, a get-together at Columbia University for "El Pasoans in Exile," not far from their apartment on the Upper Westside. Tamales, flautas, margaritas. Even a norteño band would play. It wasn't that she missed the border too much, and she wasn't even from El Paso. San Eli was on the outskirts of the outskirts of El Paso; at its worst, crumbly adobe houses with kerosene stoves, at its best, those who survived crumbly adobe houses with kerosene stoves. But Galilea thought the Columbia event was odd, from home and not from home, right on the Upper Westside. She was curious. Ben was busy traveling to Abu Dhabi for a skyscraper project. Galilea almost decided against the mixer when she saw the photo of the organizer, a consultant with emergency-red clown lips, and navy-blue eye shadow, and pencil-thin, painted-in eyebrows—Marisela Rodarte was a Mexican version of that creepy hacker Anonymous. An evening at Columbia could be another waste of time, with nice but crass people with little clue about making it in New York. And what great advice could Galilea give? A person made it in New York for the briefest of moments, before the fiction of one's life cracked against the stinky (and expensive) side streets of Broadway? Before Hoboken became a good-enough haven to retire?

"Web design? That's something I know nothing about. I spend my time in another time, one hundred years ago, with Zapata and Villa, with Carranza outmaneuvering the Centaur of the North, and battles still fought on horseback. It's an escape, I know. But I'd rather have my head there, than here. Tell me what you do. You're one of the few with half-a-brain around here."

Galilea liked his roughness, his jabbing fingers, the size of the man. At least six two and still in shape, about her age, maybe a few years younger. He reminded her of a large New York cop, beefy. Yes, that would be the word. Beefy.

She also noticed the ring on his finger, but she didn't care. She had hers too, and he didn't seem to care either. He talked softly, but with a deep baritone. They were just having a good time, talking. This Carlos, he smelled like a clean cotton shirt fresh out of the dryer. What happened to a marriage after the children left was that you could not ignore the other adult at home anymore, you could not turn away, or perhaps, the trick was to turn away without thinking you were losing your self-identity, or could be. Carlos Garcia certainly ignored everyone around them. Was he friendly with anyone else there? He certainly didn't know Galilea, and they became an odd couple amid the ear-splitting oompah-ooompah of the norteño band, and Marisela Anonymous shaking everyone's hands, and ignoring everyone too, in her pretend way as the master of ceremonies, when she was the least interesting person in the room. He was broad-shouldered, yes, and intelligent, and vigorous. Like an important politician, or a general, or a popular history professor adored by his many young students. Galilea? Petite, cute—she still jogged five miles every other day, with a yoga class Tuesdays and Saturdays—still young in her heart, still wanting…even if her dearest Benjamin couldn't, or wouldn't, anymore.

"I know this place, a couple of subway stops away, near 86th Street. French Roast. Open twenty-four hours, and the food is decent. These tamales? They call this Mexican food? They'll never get it right in New York. Galilea? What a great name, by the way."

She had noticed the thinness of the tamales—where was the *meat* inside this *masa*—but at the mixer she wasn't eating anything either, after her big kale salad with tofu, shredded cheddar, cranberries, and flax seeds in her empty apartment. Galilea was on her second margarita, and yes, she knew French Roast. About five blocks from their apartment. But she let Carlos lead the way. Men liked to think they were in charge.

It wasn't long before they mentioned their spouses, at a table behind the mirrored pillar and away from the windows on Broadway. Galilea seemed to float above her body, she the agent to her actions, but also watching herself stare at Carlos, watching herself ask him to ask her, without words, to take another step. By this point in her life, Galilea Rivero remembered so little of that life on the border she had abandoned long ago, the familia in tow, with its expectations and Old-World morality, with too much respect for authority and too quick to humble oneself to failures and disappointments with an *así es*, everything-is-in-the-hands-of-God fatalism. She wasn't into being too self-aware, and she wasn't into thinking it mattered. In this way, she had never quite fit in San Elizario. She was into today, today was New York—today was this murky darkness amid mirrors and candlelight. Even 9/11 was yesterday, New York almost free of its unforgettable past, also always remaking itself. The New York normal was this coldness in the air. What else could matter? Maybe nothing else, even if she didn't quite realize it.

"Galilea, what are you thinking? Do I invite strangers for dinner? Other women? My students? No. But you're different. You're special, I can see that. I love that look in your eyes. It takes my breath away."

Later, he continued, *"I know. I agree. I wanted to too. Wasn't sure. I just wanted to hold your hand. I'm glad that's okay. Thank you. Let's go someplace. I know. You are right. Not your apartment. I know, you are being very honest, Galilea. Thank you. You are a breath of fresh air. But I wouldn't have suggested that either, even if nobody was home. It's better to be careful, not to have doormen talking or neighbors watching. There's a hotel nearby, the Lucerne, at 79th and Amsterdam. I've had a visiting professor stay there once. Let me call them."*

Through a one-foot gap in the heavy maroon drapes, Galilea stared out the sealed corner window, at the New York night breached by the river of headlights on Amsterdam Avenue. The faint light glowed on the curtains, illuminating folds like miniature peaks and valleys. It was an opening to the outside, but also to the shelter within. She heard the door close behind her and waited for him. Without a word, Carlos came up behind her, bent down, and kissed her lips and neck. In a few more seconds, they were on the bed, her blouse and bra were off, and Galilea was on top of him.

"Ay, mi preciosa. I was dying, mi reina. I was dying. Yes. And now, it's as

if you've thrown water on a parched plant. No, no. You're gorgeous. No, I don't think they're too small. That's ridiculous. They're perfect. What deliciously brown skin. What—? Yes… Would love that. Everything. We have hours. Let me first explore every bit of you, mi reina. Let me just take my time with you."

"You want me to make you a salad for dinner? How was your trip?" Galilea heard the door open and the grainy drone of the roller-board across the herringbone wood floor. Her workout clothes were still drying in the girls' bathroom.

She had returned from the Lucerne last night with enough time to catch the last yoga class at their co-op. Her black panties were buried deep inside the hamper in the master bathroom. She had showered very late, and again this morning, even though the clover-amber scent of Dial soap still lingered on her skin. Before stepping into the shower, Galilea had picked up her panties from the hamper and inhaled their musky scent again. Jets of water closed her eyelids. Her brown skin tingled. A pleasant soreness to her muscles and nerves had released her from the ground toward a dark, watery forest.

"A salad would be great," Benjamin said, finding Galilea in the galley kitchen. He wanted a kiss, and she obliged, even if the soft goodness of his face seemed mildly revolting. She even hugged him and pulled him tight against her body. "Let me just unpack and get into shorts." As soon as she was alone in the kitchen again, Ocistar curled himself around her legs and pointed at his dish with a stare. Galilea opened a plastic pouch in a cabinet and pinched out a cylindrical "fish cookie" for the cat.

Ben had worn his black basketball shorts the first time they met. Galilea had stopped in front of Emily Dickinson's grave in the Amherst cemetery, not because she loved the poet but because she was curious. No one was around. The air carried an autumn chill that had pleasantly shocked her like finding one's path interrupted by a marching band. Her sneakers crunched on the brown, yellow, and red blanket of leaves. She stretched her legs against the wrought iron fence protecting the grave, her leg muscles bulging from the black Lycra pants that wrapped and stretched over her skin to pep up her jogging from and to UMass.

Benjamin Friedman stumbled to a stop behind her, and she caught him staring at her ass. Around his waist hung loose black shorts—an odd pair, what a ten-year-old would wear—he also on a jog, he also from UMass, but not much of a runner, huffing even minutes after introducing himself, a hand gripped on the fence, cheeks red, white and cold. He loved Emily Dickinson. Even recited a short poem to Galilea, which she thought was cute, if geeky. But that's not why she didn't utter, "Great. Have a good run," and escape quickly, as she would have with most strange men in that situation, inside a graveyard alone, in her black stretchy pants. His eyes kept her from fleeing. These plaintive, vulnerable blue eyes. A kindness manifest in them. Those had been, and still were, Benjamin Friedman's eyes. Kind, meek, and maybe fearful *of her*, which prompted her to relax as they ambled back to UMass together. Isn't it odd that often you become most vulnerable to someone when he or she does not threaten you?

Benjamin was a good boyfriend. In bed, he was gentle and rough enough for her, and he adored Galilea, for days, whenever she gave him head. He was grateful, such a pleasant surprise from her other boyfriends from San Eli and UMass who had also stared at her ass and imagined gymnastic fantasies with her when she was incapable of a steady handstand. What was it with contortionists and the imaginations of men? Galilea did adore her tight, petite body, and so did many of her friends. But the gap between what they desired of an Other and what they could actually accomplish in bed was always a chasm, sadly.

Ben was smart, with a certain literalness that transformed too many conversations into digressions on logic and the correct position of pronouns in a sentence. This amused Galilea at first until she realized this was the only way his mind worked. He would have been a good lawyer, but became an architect to distance himself from the life of his Orthodox Jewish father, another self-involved patriarch who lavished time mentoring young female Jewish lawyers not his wife.

"Anything exciting happen around here? I think we got that job in Dubai. More travel coming up this year."

"No, too quiet. Missed you." Galilea's phone vibrated in her jeans pocket against her thigh. She ignored it.

"You know, on the plane," Ben stared at his wife, halting for a moment, "I had a pain down there. The same as before."

"Jesus. Go see your doctor tomorrow." The plates in her hand suddenly rocked from side to side, and Galilea lost track of her feet and almost stepped on Ocistar. She found her way to the table and put the plates down. "I mean it. Tomorrow, Ben. No excuses. I mean, you think…"

"Prostate cancer again. You can say it. I'm not afraid of the words, but I can't take the chemo again. I might have a heart attack. I've reached the limit on certain chemo drugs."

"It's been five years. Five years, Ben. Let's take it one step at a time. Let's find out what it is. Let's not panic. Didn't he do the tests a year ago?" At the dinner table, they sat across from each other, next to a window overlooking the Hudson River.

"You mean the marker tests? To see if they could detect any more cancer in my body?"

"Yes, I guess. They were clear, weren't they?" Galilea placed her hand on his forearm as he ate his salad. She could hear only the soft whoosh of traffic and an occasional faint honk high above the streets of New York. Galilea had once loved this soft hum of the city, when high-school Livia or Emma had stretched out on a couch to study before finals, when all four of them could sleep as late as they wanted on Sundays. Lately, with the girls gone, with Ben often traveling, this near nothingness had become unnerving and in the night reared in front of her face like an invisible basilisk, and in this new now, struck at her throat, choking her. Her cell phone vibrated silently inside her jeans pocket again.

"Yes, they were. I'll call Krausner tomorrow, I promise. You know…"

"What?"

"I miss you. I miss getting inside you."

"It's okay. I mean it. It's okay," Galilea said, tears sliding over her cheeks. The salad in front of her seemed full of worms. "You can't. I understand. I love you."

"I miss you so much," Ben said, also in tears. He wiped his face on his sleeve, but kept eating. She noticed the white softness to his cheeks that had meant one thing to her years ago. "And now this. Now, maybe again. But I don't care about that. I'll see Krausner, and we'll find out what's going on. But on the plane, the only thing I thought about was how often we would make love in college, before the girls arrived, even after… How often, how delicious."

"I love you. I will always love you, no matter what."

"I miss you. Every bit of you. Every inch."

"I love you, Benjamin. I do."

"Can we, tonight? Can we do what we can do?"

"Yes, *mi precioso*. Anything for you. I am still yours."

After Ben was asleep—after, well, whatever—Galilea looked for her cell phone in the dark. She had glanced at it as she undressed, as she had waited for Ben in the bed. Galilea had powered it down to avoid any more vibrations on the bookshelf. Five texts in two hours! He wanted to see her again. *Yes, Galilea. Just like that, my darling.* He was desperate to see her again. Stupid, somewhat adolescent texts. *Galilea, my god, Galilea, I can't—Yes, that's perfect. Right there.* As she read them more carefully with the bathroom door locked, Galilea noticed the details, the language, what was said and not said between the words. Nothing for an entire day. Then five texts in an hour. Carlos. He wanted an answer from her. He was hungry for her. She decided to keep her cell phone powered down from now on, even when Ben was asleep. She would not give Carlos any answers. Too much and not enough were happening now.

They were meeting on a park bench. Galilea knew a spot right at the Hudson River, after the underpass at 95th Street. She had told Carlos to meet her there. The sunset was always gorgeous at about seven in the evening, a certain achy beauty had always attracted Galilea to those benches near the underpass: it was like allowing someone into a corner of her life that was hers, and hers alone. The shimmery silver field of the river flowed in front of her, and she always imagined adventures, a pirate ship sailing out to the Atlantic, to pillage, to escape, or she imagined a submarine surging from the waves and torpedoing the towering pylons of the George Washington Bridge. She would harbor this spot by not telling Carlos, or anyone else, that she always returned there. Men had never known everything, and that most women already knew. The savvy women didn't give a damn, one way or another. Real women used this male vanity to their advantage.

"You can't keep texting me."

"I just want to see you again."

"When the time is right."

"I loved being with you," Carlos said, placing his hand on her knee. A barge slowly cut through the dark river water, heading north.

She brushed his hand away, without looking at him. A few walkers hurried on the uneven black asphalt, all of them avoiding a sinkhole in the middle of the path that collapsed into the river. No one looked at them. Galilea imagined herself crumbling into the river with the rocks and earth, and finding a raft, and floating away along the coastline, perhaps south.

"What's wrong?"

"Nothing's wrong. I'll text you in a few days when I'm free. When I can. I like fucking you," Galilea said.

"Really? Is that's what we're doing?"

"What did you think we were doing?"

"Well, yes. But I, I…could breathe again. Like I belonged with you. Like I should've always been with you. Like I took a wrong turn and found you. Everything seemed right, for once," Carlos said.

"You're married, and I'm married. Me, happily, by the way."

"So why, then?"

"You can say it, 'Why did you fuck me?' Doesn't bother me."

"I don't know, the word, it seems so…crass. Like it means nothing."

"I enjoyed fucking you," Galilea said. "You enjoyed fucking me. I mean, we're not in El Paso anymore, that kind of thinking is even more San Eli. More rural Texas, that mexicano morality. Don't live there anymore. You don't either."

"What if I want more than just 'to fuck you'? What if that's not enough for me?"

"What is it with you? Isn't that what most men want? I'm giving it to you. I'm giving it to me. I'm happy that way."

"You never answered my question. Why?"

"That's a long story. My story…for now. I'll text you in a few days, okay?"

"I'll be waiting for you."

They walked on the asphalt pathway littered with plastic water bottles and crushed soda cans, through the paint-peeling walls of the 96th Street underpass. As they ascended to Riverside Park, Carlos caressed her shoulder, and she let his hand linger on her elbow until she squeezed his hand gently and pulled away. At the two-way path for joggers and bicyclists, they parted with a quick wave. As soon as Galilea saw Carlos disappear up the black stone stairs to Riverside

Drive, she found another bench in the park, next to bicyclists speeding on the dual asphalt pathways of this elevated swath to the park, to witness the rest of the sunset. The benches up there were not as private as the ones right in front of the Hudson River, and she could not smell the wild water, but the sunset lasted longer. A little further north, at that elevation, Civil-War cannons pointed to the river, still ready to defend the Union. But today they were only inert, cement-filled monuments. Had they ever been fired in battle?

For almost two years, Galilea had been alone, and whether it mattered, or not, wasn't important. It simply was the way it was. For day upon day, the Hudson River had kept cutting into the earth, at the same time eroding and creating the coastline.

Galilea returned from her run along the river. Entering her apartment, she ripped open the bank statement and read the total deposits, which included a payment from the insurance company. She slowly slid her body on the apartment's steel door until she plopped on the floor, blocking the entrance, Ocistar whiffing her sneakers for their strange new smell, she running her fingers through her hair, half-astonished, exhausted. From her strange vantage point on the floor, Galilea stared at the remnants of the sunset through the window and breathed deeply for what seemed the first time that day and petted her curious cat. She closed her eyes and remembered what she had seen a few seconds earlier in the bank statement: an incredible $1.4 million dollars from Ben's term-life insurance his architectural firm had offered to all their employees, which he had paid faithfully. Tonight she would call Livia and Emma, and tell them to send her all their college loans: Galilea would pay them in full, and they could go on with their lives. The girls would be responsible for graduate school, if they quit their so-so jobs and embraced that decision for themselves, but at least they would be free of college debt. Galilea would tell them what their father had done for them. She would give him all the credit. After their father had died, the girls still called their mother every week or two, but these calls seemed perfunctory. Galilea wasn't as important as their boyfriends, the new normal of the new normal.

The bills from the hospital and doctors had stopped arriving in the mail. Everyone, as far as Galilea knew, was paid, including the credit cards she had maxed out to pay for Ben's surgery. This was what was left, a little less after she paid the girls' college bills. One million dollars in New York, it wasn't nothing, but it wasn't rich. It was a cushion of a few years, if she was somehow incapable of getting out of bed, which she wasn't, and she didn't intend to be. Her website design work paid the bills—electric, co-op maintenance, groceries, and even an occasional short vacation to Florida to watch the sea. She had not been back to Texas for years. That million dollars, if she could grow it, would be her retirement, her cushion in case of an emergency, perhaps even a small legacy to leave any grandchildren. But Galilea suspected only some of this money would be left, because nothing ever happened as one expected it.

She had never expected Ben to die in surgery. Galilea had imagined he would fight his new cancer after surgery with whatever chemo drugs he could still tolerate. Yet, because he died so quickly, that was why she had money left and why Galilea didn't need to sell their co-op or take other emergency measures to survive without further burdening her girls or anyone else. That was why she didn't have to return to San Eli or Wooster or Fresno. Dearest, merciful Ben.

She had never expected to be living in New York, after being born in San Elizario on the Mexican-American border, an afterthought of El Paso, which was itself on the edge of the edge of the United States, still swooning to the Chi-lites, Minnie Riperton, and Peaches & Herb. Yet, because she had left the border, she had found the Hudson River, she designed websites with a creative edge, and she did not have to explain herself, or what she did, to anybody. In New York, as long as one paid the bills and was relatively quiet, nobody cared what god a person followed, if she followed any god, what religion she practiced, if any, or what she did at night, if she did anything at all. If one loved sex, one could enjoy it. If one liked to experiment, one could do that too. If a person liked the Jewish baker on Amsterdam and 87th Street, liked the bread, not the gay man behind the counter, well, she could spread butter on that seed-encrusted health loaf every week, if she wanted. New York was freedom, New York was solitude, and on a few nights the City descended into loneliness. The key was always to remember the next day.

I need to see you, Galilea. Please. Her cell phone vibrated in her jeans again as she walked out her apartment door, freshly showered, here and not here, wanting to move again, her muscles sore, wanting, wanting, still wanting…

Galilea had been at the river a few hours ago, on her jog. Yet there she was again, on the bench, watching that tempestuous water slice through the earth with its endless power. Past lovers often wanted to return to the same emotional plateau, to the same ephemeral connection, even years later, even if for her that connection had been only a moment, a salve, an escape, a whimsy, a respite, an action unexplainable, and with luck, an annihilating pleasure. But she knew that already, she had always known that. What had been missing was what came afterward, if anything or everything.

Near her sneaker, half underneath the bench, a shiny, metallic edge caught her eye. It looked like the edge of a Kennedy half-dollar. Did it slip out of someone's pocket? In the red-orange light of the sunset, the edge shimmered like a tiny half-moon abandoned. Galilea picked up the piece, thin and bendable, a perfect circle—the top to a yogurt container?—and studied the faded lettering, still visible under the dust. With her thumb she wiped it clean: *Arethusa*. Greek? A new, or very old, yogurt company? She imagined what the word could mean, and back in her apartment she would look it up. But there it was, an idea. She twisted the thick, grainy aluminum in her hand and watched the sun glint off the silver. The Mediterranean. Livia would adore having Ocistar for a week or two. Perhaps an off-season rental near the sea. Another chance for anything and everything.

FACE TO FACE

Early on Sunday evening, the temperature had dropped drastically, even for late February in Manhattan. After just the short walk to Fairway Market, the culinary Mecca of Manhattan's Upper West Side, Ricky Quintana was panting, his asthma clogging up his lungs, his face, which his girlfriend Marisa claimed appeared more Greek than Chicano, so numb he had to wait a few seconds inside the market before consciousness seeped up from deep inside his cold skull to his eyes, to the blonde with her hair pinned up in a tight bun and perfectly arched eyebrows as she jostled past him in a chocolate mink, to the items on his grocery list. Julio Gonzales from Guanajuato was perched on a stepladder arranging the uncannily shiny Honey Crisp apples in a pyramid, and Ricky for a moment thought about saying hello, but Julio was busy and out of reach. At their first meeting, Julio had asked Ricky, "You mean, *como el esposo de Lucy?*" *El güero* with the mustache, who could be an asshole with his trabajadores and turn on a dime and smile pleasantly if one was wearing the latest Patagonia jacket over a light salmon Oxford shirt, was also prowling the vegetable aisles to keep them clear for the men with dollies racing into Fairway from the double-parked trucks with boxes of asparagus, carrots, scallions, giant California oranges, and arugula. The to-and-fro, Ricky noticed, left a trail of sawdust that, with each gust of arctic air, disappeared from the dark sidewalk on Broadway. The stocky Julio, an illegal—as were most of the workers who minded the gigantic produce department—had a few months ago declared to Ricky in Spanish, "At least I'm not at the warehouse anymore! They work you like an animal over there."

As Ricky marched in and out of the aisles to get what he liked to eat—Red Delicious apples, extra-large navel oranges, St. Lucien brie, calamata olives, Fairway's piñon nut pesto sauce—he glanced at his friend Julio and the other trabajadores at Fairway. Those who had seen him occasionally chat with Julio grinned silently at Ricky. Others just ignored him, stoic, busy, on the lookout for *el güero*. Ricky noticed Julio's ragged, leathery face was lost in thought, and Ricky wondered what had happened to Julio's sixteen-year-old niece, whom Julio had recently told him was probably pregnant by *"un pinche puertorriqueño,"* a niece, along with her boyfriend, whom Julio wanted to kill. When the squat Julio had blurted out the news to Ricky, it had been an uncomfortable revelation for Julio, and for their easy, usually pleasant conversations at Fairway, from *"¿Como está ahora, señor?"* and *"¡Qué bonito día nos tocó!"* and *"¿Está seguro que usted, señor, es mexicano? ¡Es el más alto mexicano en Nueva York!"* and *"¡Debe de tener usted buen trabajo y estudios, porque aquí se me hace la comida muy cara!"* to the tears that welled up in Julio's tired gray eyes as he revealed this bitter disappointment, this loss of hope, for his brother's daughter, Maribel.

Was he—Ricky thought weeks after this exchange—still like these mexicanos? Julio's white stubble on his dry cheeks, the soft, nameless, faded baseball cap on his head, the way Julio moved from fruit to fruit in a semi-hunch, determined to do his work above all else, routinely deferential to any customer who crossed his path, really, sheepish, and excessively kind—all these things reminded Ricky of his abuelito. Ricky remembered how he had worked for his grandfather in grade school and high school in Ysleta, cutting grass on Colonel Smith's farm, planting flowers in the spring in Socorro, Texas, whitewashing the gigantic cottonwoods next to the irrigation canals, Saturday after Saturday. Ricky remembered the calluses on his abuelito's puffy knuckles and yet how happy Don José always was to be under the sun at lunchtime, reclining against the dry banks of the canal, at times peacefully asleep. Their exchanges: "Why don't you ask Colonel Smith for more money?" and the retort, "*Ay, mi hijo*, I have what I need. It's good to know what you need or else you end up chasing your own tail, like Lobo." Ricky, the teenager, had made it a point to get out of Ysleta, out of El Paso, to ask for more, to risk failure for success, and to apply to colleges across the Eastern seaboard. When Merrill Lynch recruited him five years ago from NYU, and he had signed the lease on his Upper West Side apartment, Ricky believed he had taken an irrevocable leap beyond the Chihuahuan desert of the Mexican-American border, beyond his father and mother, who begged him to return home whenever he mentioned he was lonely, beyond begging for help from anybody, beyond depending on the good graces of others, especially gringos, toward self-achievement, to demanding what he wanted, to expanding, even, his ideas of what he could possibly desire. Ricky Quintana had escaped Ysleta, yet, every Sunday afternoon or evening, after he saw Julio Gonzales in the fruit aisles at Fairway, Ysleta would invade Ricky's mind like an uneasy spirit that refused to die: he couldn't help Julio, he wanted to help Julio, he was like Julio, and he was not like Julio anymore and perhaps never would be.

At the checkout lane, which was so narrow that Ricky had to turn sideways to avoid bumping into the Belgian chocolate squares and the cracker-like pale orange sponges in row upon neat row on impulse-buy racks, the Jamaican or possibly Antiguan checker snarled at him and dragged his groceries on the electronic scanner and tossed them into a grocery bag and waited with an open hand and a red-eyed, somnolent stare at the space above his head as Ricky signed the credit card slip. Once, Ricky had questioned the scanned price on a bag of pre-washed spinach, and this checker had dramatically summoned the manager and grumbled something about *"espece d'imbeciles"* slowing down the checkout lines and threw Ricky this look that seemed to split his head open like a machete. Ricky had been right, but who cared if he had been right? Since then, this checker (who was indeed the fastest) hated his guts or appeared to loathe his very presence, Ricky now the oppressor in her eyes, the disgusting, tall, white yuppie, the one who symbolized her abysmally low pay, her pressure-filled minutes, the simultaneous near and far of what and who she was not.

Finally in his apartment again, Ricky locked his steel door and put away his groceries in the kitchen that was no bigger than his bathroom and slumped into the sofa. He could hear the Broadway traffic echo through his massive window, the whistle of the winter wind, and the creaks that seemed to emanate from his fireplace or beyond it. He walked into his pitch-black bedroom and flipped on the light, and of course no one was there. No one was also in the bathroom. No one lurked behind his shower curtain. Ricky Quintana was alone in this warm, shadowy darkness above the lights of Broadway. A shiver trembled up his spine. He turned on the TV and flipped to the cable news channel's *America's Watch*, which was still running retrospectives on Armstrong Ferry, the causes he had taken up over the years, his unrelenting, three-year attacks against illegal immigrants to the United States, hour-upon-hour of "news" filled with Ferry's red-faced diatribes, his asking a "question" of a guest only to rudely interrupt and answer his own question with more simplistic, incendiary pronouncements, Ferry's smile mocking of any view, any group, any person who did not immediately recognize his greatness, his rightness, his "impeccable logic." In fact, when Armstrong Ferry grinned to silently disgrace anybody who dared to counter him or his arguments, Ricky thought it looked as if Ferry wanted to eat them. The TV light intermittently illuminated the darkness like faraway thunderbolts, and Ricky began to masturbate to mental images of Marisa Yoshimoto, to making love to her again soon, to watching her head grind into his pillow in ecstasy. But at once Ricky stopped: it was better with the real thing, it was better with her scent and her softness at his fingertips, there was no need to rely on faraway images for a false ecstasy, he had but to ask Marisa for her to say yes to him, to metamorphose his dream into reality, to turn the suspense of a fictional mystery into the thrill of the sweetest annihilation, to escape and fly free. The TV images kept bursting into the darkness of the living room, illuminating the night as well as obscuring it.

"The Mexican culture is fundamentally incompatible with American culture, and we're just importing their poverty and the poverty of their values! Our government refuses to secure our borders, and where has that left us? Higher crime by illegal aliens who have already demonstrated no respect for the law! Higher high school dropout rates as Hispanic students, their parents, and entire communities refuse to learn English! An education bureaucracy that shoves bilingual education and multiculturalism down our throats! America is still vulnerable at our borders, years after terrorists invaded this country and killed thousands on 9/11!

"But, Senator, I just have to laugh at your arguments. Racism? This is not about racism, Senator. It's simply about what's right. The white middle class in this country has been abandoned by your pro-NAFTA polices, by a government which simply refuses to aid local communities fighting against the deluge of illegal aliens sucking up resources, on welfare, in the hospital emergency rooms, in schools where our own children are receiving a substandard education! Now you're arguing about the rights of illegal aliens? You should be ashamed!

"Deport them! Door-to-door if necessary! Get the Army to patrol our borders! Give INS the resources to do it! We can't start talking about anything, and certainly never about amnesty for illegals, until our borders are secure! We are losing our way of life! We are losing the achievements, let me add, of the white, Anglo-Saxon, Protestant, European immigrants, who I admit, may or may not have arrived here illegally, yes, but that's not the point. That's a red herring. Today's massive illegal immigration from Latin America is overwhelming us. This country needs to get serious about stopping it before it's too late!"

Long ago, Ricky had seethed at these words that emanated every night from his television set, right at about dinnertime when he would flip through the cable channels and stop at *America's Watch* to torture himself by listening to Armstrong Ferry. This warbly, deep-throated voice, unleashed, unopposed, even encouraged and lauded by small-town mayors, Minutemen with microphones in the no-man's-land of the Arizona desert, self-selected viewers who also ranted against illegals and waved a metaphorical American flag in honor of *America's Watch*. *How could a major news network, these sponsors, allow this moron on a supposed "news" show night after night?* Ricky had thought, gritting his teeth. *Ferry's not calling us spics, but he might as well be. He reduces us to stereotypes, he picks the worst portrayals, the scandalous examples, and applies these images to everybody, to all Latinos, illegal or not. And they let him. And they have been letting him do it for years. Let's not talk about what the English and the Dutch did to the Algonquin in New York. Let's not talk about slavery, what about those "great values?" English immigrants, Irish immigrants, Italian immigrants, Jewish immigrants, they just came and they took, and there was no legal or illegal! It's bullshit! And they simply let him do it night after night.*

Tonight, however, Ricky Quintana just smiled at Ferry's words — only words now, the man gone — and added an extra dollop of pesto sauce to his pasta and more grated Pecorino cheese. He turned off the television and listened to the wind, for any noise, and for the first time in a long while, Ricky believed he belonged in New York.

One morning three weeks ago an innocuous decision had changed everything for Ricky Quintana. Since returning from visiting his father and mother in El Paso for Christmas — tamales, *buñuelos, arroz con leche, champurrado* — Ricky decided to walk to work in Midtown, to Merrill Lynch's research division on 50th Street, right before Park Avenue. That Monday, a wintry blast from Canada left the cracked sidewalks on Broadway slippery with muddy snow, and Ricky woke up early, knowing his walk would take extra time, and trudged south toward Columbus Circle and the fancy Time Warner Center, at which point he would decide whether to turn on 59th Street, toward the Apple cube store next to FAO Schwartz, or to continue south on Broadway to 50th Street, just before Times Square, and then have his cup of coffee at a Starbucks. His blood pressure was borderline high, his triglycerides were twice normal—his doctor had warned him at his annual December checkup—and Ricky needed to avoid alcohol and sugar, and to exercise every day, if he could. But that day he never reached Columbus Circle on foot.

At 63rd Street and Broadway, right after the Sony IMAX and Gracious Living stores, Ricky's lungs had enough of the bitter cold, and he couldn't breathe, but he remembered passing a Starbucks on Amsterdam, behind the Barnes and Noble superstore in front of him. He hurried into the coffee shop, found the restroom, ensconced in one far corner, miraculously vacant, and immediately inhaled two puffs of Primatene Mist, which he always carried with his laptop. In line for his Venti Mild, Ricky could feel his lungs expanding, his heavy wheeze receding, the blood coming back to his head and clearing his mind. That's when he saw him. At the front of the line and already paying for his coffee. The clarity of this man stunned Ricky: *there* he was, as real as real can be. Others at that Starbucks, which Ricky had never been to before, also staring, one woman pointing to another with a subway map—tourists—and barely able to contain her glee at spotting a famous personality. Ricky had seen Harrison Ford strolling on Broadway. One night he had sat next to Richard Dreyfus for a few stops on a downtown No. 1 subway. And then, for about twelve blocks, he had even shared a bench-seat with Frances McDormand on the M104 bus. And like most New Yorkers, Ricky never did anything or said anything, but simply returned to minding his business. But Ricky Quintana had never been face to face with this famous reporter before. When the reporter, instead of leaving, wiggled onto a stool next to the corner of the bathroom and snapped his newspaper open, Ricky decided to linger in the warmth of this Starbucks.

Sitting next to a small table a few feet away, Ricky noticed the sandy-haired, somewhat-heavier-than-expected reporter sip his coffee for a few minutes, pop a pill from an open black portfolio at his feet, and altogether ignore everyone else at the Starbucks. "Plavix," Ricky read as the plastic bottle was left momentarily on the counter. Others, except for the tourists who were walking out the door, also ignored each other, and read newspapers or typed on their Blackberrys or iPhones. Outside on the street, on Amsterdam, Ricky focused for the first time on the television studio for the cable news network, the double glass doors constantly swinging open with a shiny flash, and many workers rushing across the street right into the Starbucks. After about fifteen minutes, the reporter—whose hair was also much thinner and stiffer than Ricky expected, almost Donald-Trump-like— abruptly left the coffee shop and marched into the television studios and disappeared behind a set of heavy wooden doors framed by two guards in red blazers. Ricky would have been late had he continued his walk to his office at Merrill Lynch, but he hailed a cab and arrived just in time.

In Ricky's head, for days after that non-encounter, he imagined shoving the reporter from behind into the traffic on Amsterdam, he imagined stabbing the moron in the neck with a pen, he imagined, he imagined…but he had done nothing. Each night, as more words and their images assaulted him from his Sony again, as he sat there and ate his dinner alone, sometimes distracting himself by thinking of Marisa, Ricky hated himself for having done nothing. This hate overwhelmed him and only seemed to sharpen his sense of outrage at what he heard, at his missed opportunity, at his own cowardice, at the cowardice of everyone across the country who heard what he heard night after night but did nothing, lifted not one finger, for Julio, for his abuelitos, for his mother and father, for anyone who did not deserve these lies in the name of the God of High Ratings, for the voiceless who could not respond to these well-worded distortions, these self-serving provocations masquerading as intelligent arguments. Ricky hated himself until, one day, on his way to work again, he returned to that Starbucks on Amsterdam. Returned again the next day, and waited anxiously, when the reporter did not appear as he had that first morning. And *there* he was! Perhaps the reporter was not there every day, Ricky reasoned, but only a few times a week.

Ricky quickly found the news item through a Google search, the reason why *America's Watch* had had a substitute anchor for a few weeks last summer. One major pharmaceutical company—a giant with seventy-percent gross profit margins—along with a smaller rival, were the two makers of stents for opening up clogged arteries to the heart, an incredibly profitable business Ricky was intimately familiar with at Merrill Lynch. But the pharma giant took it a step further: it also manufactured the drug Plavix to correct the blood-clot problem that plagued many stents, a delicious paradox not uncommon in this industry, which Ricky admired, of a company making money to correct the shortcomings or mistakes of this selfsame company's products. Heads I win; tails you lose. At a vitamin shop, Ricky scoured the shelves until he found small, round, rose-colored pills that best matched the bestselling anti-blood-clot drug. In his hand, the tiny caplets felt like dynamite.

At the Starbucks, early this time, and at the appropriate seat, close to the bathroom but with a stool free next to him, between him and the dark corner into the bathroom, Ricky Quintana waited, his nose deep inside *The New York Times*—waited until, until, yes, the opportunity appeared again, a second chance, yes, the perfect chance. The creature of habit seemed in a hurry to meet his destiny. The reporter shoved open the Starbucks glass doors, dropped his black portfolio to save the stool next to Ricky's, and as the reporter waited in the back of the long line, away from the dark corner and any possibility of getting a clear glance at it, Ricky stood up, as if searching his jacket pockets and so blocking anybody's view of the reporter's portfolio, reached in, grabbed the medicine bottle, and sat down again. In a few seconds, his black North Face jacket open and providing more cover, Ricky poured out the Plavix and poured in the vitamin pills. His heart thumping inside his chest like a trapped, enraged *duende*, Ricky stood up again, dropped the medicine bottle back into the portfolio, and picked up his coffee and started for the door. He imagined Armstrong Ferry's huge, soft body lunging at him like an old albino bear, outraged, that familiar pale face blushing and demanding an explanation. Ricky imagined others pointing him out. But not one pair of eyes even bothered to look his way as Ricky shoved open the Starbucks doors and strode around the corner, into a cab, away. This was New York.

As the taxi sped around the statue of Christopher Columbus atop a granite pillar, the explorer seemed more like an Oxford don rather than an adventurer for slaves and gold, suspended amid the space created by the glass skyscrapers around him. Ricky reached behind him and pulled straight the cobalt blue jacket of his Halston suit to avoid too many wrinkles and tightened the knot of his red-patterned Ferragamo tie and stared through the vague reflection of himself to the blur of yellow taxis and pedestrians in black and gray winter coats beyond the taxi's window. He and New York City were meant to be together.

The St. Lucien brie was next to the fancy spelt crackers from Iceland, and the acrid whiff of the calamata olives even occasionally reached his bedroom. Ricky Quintana's fingers nervously slipped and skipped over the keys of his black MacBook, his fingernails too long, as he returned an email (on a Sunday night!) from his boss at Merrill Lynch who wanted to know when the year-end quarterly report for consumables in the biotech sector would be ready. Ricky's report was already a week late, and he had never been late delivering a report before, but nobody else would or could do it in late February. He was it.

"Hey, Rick, come over here!" He heard Marisa's high-pitched, he-still-thought-sexy voice from his living room as his quivery pinky hit the delete button repeatedly to correct his mistakes. In fact, it had been Marisa Yoshimoto's voice, with its squeaky, come-hither quality, that had tickled him in that special place one night less than nine months ago, at the Parlour, an Irish pub on 86th Street and Broadway. Ricky had been attending a birthday party for an analyst buddy also at Merrill Lynch, and he had overheard, above the reverberating cover of Bonnie Raitt's "Something To Talk About," above even the chirps of the Ms. Pac-Man/Galaxaga machine behind him that had momentarily reminded him of his days in El Paso and Riverside High School, this lilting laugh, this fluttering, mesmerizing song from an otherwise unintelligible conversation. He had turned away from the bartender and the outstretched mug of Corona Light to lock eyes, for two seconds, with a slim, somewhat slight and pretty woman with chocolate brown eyes, shimmery black short hair dancing against tiny diamond earrings. And that intoxicating voice. When she smiled so gratefully, so naturally at him, her glossy lips played against her white teeth, as if ready for fun, ready to laugh, ready for mischief. It had taken Ricky less than five minutes to introduce himself to Marisa and less than five minutes after that for Marisa's girlfriend to excuse herself to search for the Parlour's restroom with a wide-eyed glance at her, and about half an hour after that for Marisa to hand Ricky her phone number—actually, she had scribbled it on his palm with another laugh that seemed to hit him like a lance to the chest. The next Friday night, they had dinner at the boisterous Gabriela's on Columbus and 93rd Street, and the rest was, well, their short history. "Hey, I wanna show you something."

But today, Ricky ignored his girlfriend for a moment, finished typing his email as the radiator gurgled, and said loudly to his MacBook, a drop of perspiration just grazing the fleshy nub outside his left ear, "I'll be there in a second! Almost done!" Ricky buried his head in his hands as he waited for the rainbow wheel of the Mac to stop spinning, to power the computer down, and he smelled it again—this briefly sharp, musty, unmistakably dead-animal scent that seemed to waft in from his window, which was open only an inch. It wasn't coming from the Astor's courtyard, he suddenly realized: it was coming from the radiator below the window. Ricky jumped up from his desk, yanked open the beige metal cover that housed the bedroom radiator of his otherwise amazing pre-war, rent-stabilized apartment—less than half a block from Fairway Market—and saw it: a mouse, its little shrunken head caved in.

"Come here," Marisa begged him sweetly from the living room, as Ricky rushed into the bathroom outside the bedroom, pushed the door half-closed, and quickly pulled a wad of toilet paper into his hand. The news blared through the open door from the Sony in the living room.

"Just one second," Ricky said as he rushed past her again, hiding the toilet paper in his palm, and hoping she wouldn't follow him into the bedroom and freak out. Marisa—still in her travel clothes after a business trip to Miami, her black pumps already abandoned like useless relics on the sky-blue Navajo rug under his slatted coffee table—seemed like a cat perched on his downy ocean of a sofa, her sleek legs tucked under her. Her back was to the bathroom as she faced the TV, which fit in an alcove two feet from the wide, six-foot-high window overlooking a rooftop on Broadway. As Ricky rolled the mouse onto the toilet paper, and the mouse's body crumpled into a curvy L on its soft white shroud, he remembered first making love to Marisa on his sofa, she rushing to shimmy out of her skirt and happy to be guided, not to the bedroom, but back onto the sofa by his hands, over the sofa's edge, into the most delicious of L's, and arching her unbelievably beautiful ass, just the right angle, just for him. That crazy Friday night—a near two-hour lovefest on the sofa, on the floor, on his bed—one of them had inadvertently smacked the coffee table and propelled the magazines and what was left of their margaritas on the jagged glyphs of the rug. Palming the now-weighty toilet paper, Ricky marched into the bathroom again, flushed the toilet, and stepped into the living room. "What's up?"

"He's dead."

"Who?"

"That guy on *America's Watch*. Armstrong Ferry. The guy who hates immigrants. Listen, they're running clips from previous shows."

"Yeah, I know," Ricky said distractedly, putting his arm under her as if suddenly cold while Marisa snuggled closer to him on the sofa. He began to kiss her neck, which smelled deliciously of Shalimar. The scent brought him back to her. She had come to Ricky's apartment straight from La Guardia. "I heard. Are we going out or staying in?"

"Didn't you hate him?"

"He was an idiot."

"Heart attack last night. I thought you'd be happy. Karma."

"Don't care anymore. I just care about this delicious sweet thing next to me, who I can undress and make love to, who keeps my motor hummin' every day of the week. I miss you. TV's got nothin' on you, *mi preciosa*." Marisa—her body, her scent, this squeaky-voiced affability— had always taken him out of his obsessions, the outrages in his head, and even now, his vague, secret fears.

"Sweetie, I'll take care of you a little later," Marisa purred into his ear, which sent a shiver up his spine. She didn't take her dark brown eyes off the television, but wiggled into the sofa as if trying to burrow into it. "You know what you do to me when you start talking Spanish."

Marisa wrapped her arms around his waist, and he traced a meandering line over her thigh.

"There he is again," Marisa continued. "No more rants against illegal aliens. Against 'the foreign invasion of our Anglo-Saxon culture.' You know, he hated the Chinese; he hated the Japanese too—anyone who was beating Americans at their own game. Not just Mexicans. He hated anyone who wasn't like him."

"Armstrong Ferry was a jerk. I really don't want to talk about him now."

"I just imagined you would be happy with the news."

"Well, what are we doing tonight? The weekend's almost gone." He pushed away. "Let's celebrate, let's do something fun, *preciosa*. Let's get outta here."

"Celebrate what?" she said, smiling hopefully, but with a quizzical look on her moon-shaped face.

"Life. Happiness. Sunday nights."

Ricky Quintana shivered from head to toe as though an electric shock coursed through his lanky body. He glanced out the window, listened intently to any sounds beyond the blathering television, possibly in the dimly lit hallway, but nothing seemed out of place. Everything was as it should be. Outside the window and beyond the rooftop, a few soft honks from the traffic wafted toward the sky.

YAMECAH

Officer Jelani Williams sat at the front desk of the 103rd Precinct in Jamaica, Queens, behind the vestibule in Plexiglass, which was behind the steel doors on the busy avenue, the sidewalk in front of which was ringed by yellow concrete pillars on the curb. Centuries before, the name of the local Algonquin tribe, Yamecah, had been anglicized by the British to Jameco and later Jamaica after they defeated the Dutch, who had bought the land by the beaver pond from the Native Americans for two guns and a coat.

A cup of coffee steamed on Officer Williams's desk, with ring binders on active cases from this week—complaints, incidents, investigations, whatever came through those doors. An old Windows computer blinked next to the binders. Behind Officer Williams loomed nine gray metal desks, with only two police officers at work. More offices, with robin-egg blue doors and wall-windows, were in the background, all empty and dark. Clipboards, lists with assignments, or announcements covered almost every surface of every wall and wall-window. The police station radiated a gritty, yet friendly quality. Against one wall, closed-circuit monitors dangled over the nine desks, watching the sidewalks in front and the garage in back.

The front steel doors swung open. Officer Williams immediately reclined in her seat: a sturdy, dark-haired woman pushed a bargain-basement stroller with a baby in it and struggled to keep the heavy doors open as she maneuvered the stroller and baby inside. Behind them followed a little girl.

"*Señora, necesito ayuda. Es urgente. Mi esposo, mi esposo—*" the woman stammered as she faced the semi-transparent Plexiglass and spoke haltingly at the police officer. Williams guessed she was another Central American immigrant from the neighborhood, short and powerfully built like the Olmec descendants on the History Channel. Once Jamaica, Queens had been an overwhelmingly African-American neighborhood. "*Me quiero separar, y me golpea. ¡Y me dijo que nos va a matar! ¡Mire lo que me hizo ayer, cuando me empujó del segundo piso de los escalones de nuestro edificio!*" The woman twisted her body to show the police officer her shoulder and neck, which were streaked with reddish scrapes and bruises.

"Wait, wait, just one second—"

"*Me llamo Ximena Garza, y soy de Guatemala, y no tengo papeles. Estoy aquí sola, y mi esposo es Julio Gonzales, mexicano, y nos conocimos en Jamaica, pero Dios mío, tanto sufrimiento me ha dado este hombre, y lo quiero dejar, pero aquí no tengo familia. Estoy sola, ¡ayúdenos! ¡Va a matar a mis hijitas! ¡Por favor! ¡No sé qué hacer! ¡No sé qué hacer!*" The trembling woman sobbed as she blurted out these words, gripping the hand of the little girl, who stared with a face of stone at the police officer. The baby in the stroller wiggled inside a pink onesie. The little girl wore a tight yellow t-shirt smeared with what appeared to be grape jelly, a rainbow of rhinestones spelling L-O-V-E across her flat chest.

"*Un momento,*" Officer Williams said, holding out her palm to the agitated woman who seemed determined, her neck stiff and shoulders squared, to get her story out. Her brown-black eyes smoldered with a mix of anger and pain against her impenetrable dark chocolate skin. "Sean, Leo, you guys know Spanish? I need help here!"

"You kiddin'?" someone called out behind her.

"Just tell her to leave the tacos and say 'thank you'!" a gravelly voice said in a thick Brooklyn accent.

"Not funny," Williams shot back, still friendly but with an edge in her voice. Years ago they had teased her for her "Washington Heights" accent.

"*¡Me va a matar, Señora Oficial! ¡A todos! Me lo dijo. Esta noche. ¡Nos va a matar! Empezo todo con mi sobrina, Maribel. Parece que estaba enamorado de ella, y tiene solamente dieciséis años! Ayúdenme, por Díos santo. ¡No sé qué hacer!*" the woman said louder, exasperated. She wiped her tears away savagely, glared at her older daughter, and pointed to the floor. "*¡Cuida a la niña! ¡No nos vamos de aquí hasta que nos ayude la policía! ¡No me importa lo que pase!*"

"Yes, we are the *policía*. Got that. That's where you are. Someone hurt you? Miss, I can't understand you. Someone push you on the street?"

"*Mi esposo sigue tomando. ¡Cada noche una borrachera! No tenemos dinero, o regresaría a Guatemala—*"

"You from Guatemala? Thought I heard you say that before—"

"*Sí, mi familia está en Guatemala. Le chismiaron sus amigos que andaba con otro, pero Salvador nomás es mi amigo. Me defiende, pero es muy tímido, el pobre.*"

"An *amigo* did this to you? Let me look at that neck and shoulder,"

Officer Williams said through the Plexiglass vestibule, pointing at her own neck and shoulder, and making a circling motion with her index finger for the woman to turn around. The woman twisted her torso again, pulled her blouse down to her maroon bra and showed Williams more of her bruised shoulder. A nasty mix of vermillion and purple bloomed on her deeply brown skin.

"*Mi esposo se llama Julio Gonzales, de Guanajuato. Trabaja en una tienda que se llama Fairway. Vivimos en Queens, casi en la esquina de Linlin y Estufin. ¡Ay Díos mío, no sé cómo pronunciar estas calles bien! Linlin y Estufin. Número 113-10 en Estufin. ¡Señora, no puedo regresar a mi casa! ¡Mi esposo es muy violento, y nos va a matar!*"

"*Número*, okay. Your amigo is *violento*. Okay," Officer Williams said, frustrated with what little she could understand. She had so much work to do. "Here, take this paper, and write it out, write out your complaint against your *amigo*," the cop continued, making a writing motion on the blank computer sheets she pushed to the woman through the slot in the Plexiglass. "Write it out with this." Williams handed the stocky woman a pen too. "Write out your *casa número*, your story, your complaint, whatever. Sit down over there," she continued, rapping brusquely against the Plexiglass and pointing at two wooden chairs in the foyer. "Sit down and write it out over there," Williams said, almost sounding angry although she wasn't, and pointing again at the chairs. "*Español*, please. Write it out."

The Guatemalan woman stood staring through the fog-like Plexiglass haze at Officer Jelani Williams for what seemed like a minute, fingering nervously the white sheets of paper and the pen in her small yet powerful hands. Finally she sat down on a chair and gripped the pen awkwardly, as her daughter waited on the floor in front of the stroller and made faces at her little sister.

Ximena Garza wrote on all four sheets of paper, wrote on both sides, wrote in a hard-to-read jagged script that wasn't proper Spanish, but more a series of colloquial phrases, sentence fragments, and misspellings. She wrote about her abusive husband and how certain she was that tonight he would kill her and their two little girls. He would kill her for wanting to leave him, for desiring to be free, for seeking a life without deep bruises or punches to the gut that took her breath away or flashes of a knife at the kitchen table. Julio would kill her because he was impossibly in love with his brother's daughter Maribel, and Ximena was only in the way. She wrote a kind of paragraph-announcement about her village in Guatemala, and how she had made the journey to New York City, even alluding to the three rapes, by strangers, she had survived along the way. A toll she had imagined was worth paying, even years later. She had traveled across a continent to reach the America of Jamaica, Queens, New York. One night she had spotted Julio Gonzales in a loud Latin dance club on Queens Boulevard. What had caught her attention was his toothy smile and powerful body, and what had kept it was the soft touch of his hand. Soon she was pregnant with Aurora. And then Beatriz.

Ximena Garza's lines on the paper were not straight, yet the pages were no longer a shock of white, but brimming with a slanted sea of ink. At the bottom, she printed her address in large block letters and numbers, near the corner of Linden and Sutphin Boulevard in Jamaica, Queens. She stared at the pages and flipped them over like brittle parchment, stared at her daughters and stared at the pages again. The woman sobbed as she reread her mishmash of words and phrases. The little girl put her hand gently on her mother's knee. The baby stared stupefied at both of them, her black coal eyes darkly brilliant against plump white cheeks, studying their pained expressions, still lost in a world without words.

"*Aquí está, Señora Oficial. Aquí está todo. No puedo regresar a mi casa, por Díos santo. Maribel tambien está en peligro.*"

"Thank you, thank you very much," Officer Williams said as she reached for the sheets of paper through the slot and scooped up the pen without taking her eyes from the computer screen in front of her. "*Gracias.*" She turned to the Guatemalan woman, grinned, and turned back to her work. From a shelf above the computer, Williams grabbed a folder, wrote a number on the label, pushed the four sheets into the folder, and dropped the folder into a metal bin on her desk. Dozens upon dozens of manila folders were stacked in that bin. Later that day, another officer would mistakenly pick up two folders from the stack, one the thin folder with Ximena Garza's story in Spanish. For a second, the officer would stare at the slanted blue hieroglyphics on the pages. He would shove that folder into a wall with thousands of precinct cases, on the bottom shelf labeled "Miscellaneous."

Officer Williams typed her reports on the computer, and for a few minutes seemed entranced by the screen. Something was not right. The bright sunshine had never flashed into the foyer from the avenue again. The metal doors to the street had never creaked open like a crypt nor slammed shut again. A deadly quiet had never been interrupted on the other side of the Plexiglass. Williams half-stood up and glanced below, through the thick plastic wall. The Guatemalan woman sat at the edge of the wooden chair, kneading her hands. Her daughter, the little warrior, still squatted on the cement floor and gently rocked the stroller back and forth a few inches. Strangely they seemed to have shrunk to an even smaller size than before, almost blending into the brown water-stained wall and radiator like a bas-relief.

"Miss. Miss!" Officer Williams said while rapping on the Plexiglass. "We'll let you know what happens. You don't have to stay here. There's nothing to wait for. *Nada*."

The Guatemalan woman stared at the blurry outline of the police officer through the Plexiglass, tried to decipher the English words for a second, and half-stood up from her chair too.

"*Sae-nyo-ra*, bye, bye," Officer Williams repeated politely, and waved an open hand to the woman. The police officer pointed at the metal doors, and waved again.

The call to the police had come from a neighbor, who heard a woman's screams and objects smashing against the walls and a child's pleas in the darkness before dawn. Two days later on the NYPD Queens website, Crime Stoppers had a grainy, ten-second video of a man stumbling through the lobby of 113-10 Sutphin Boulevard in Jamaica, after a bloody domestic scene which left one woman unconscious and her daughter in a medically induced coma. The public could submit information regarding this incident by logging onto the CrimeStoppers website at www.NYPDCrimeStoppers.com.

FRAGMENTS OF A DREAM

Maribel waited for Hector at the back of the Super 8 Jamaica North
Conduit, just a mile from JFK. La Mari had lied about her age,
and really they thought she was twenty-one, or at least they didn't
care too much, as long as she cleaned the rooms and washed the
sheets and didn't fight with *las otras viejas*. La Mari didn't talk to
the other cleaning women, and why should she? She was finishing
her sophomore year in high school, and she wasn't staying in this
hellhole for Aqueduct flunkies and their evening rendezvous with ugly,
needy women. The disgusting filth they left behind! She did her job,
collected her paycheck, worked on algebra. Most of the time she could
catch up on her homework in an empty room, and the supervisor,
a fat blond Mets fan who was too friendly with the Aqueduct boys,
let her be. Mami, she would say in her heavy Anglo accent—Scottish
or Irish or whatever—clean those bathrooms when you finish your
schoolwork, okay? Mami, you good? Then Maribel wouldn't see la
gorda for hours. Occasionally, in a hallway of the Super 8, she would
hear huffs, like cow noises, and maybe a few whispers, and Mari knew
la gorda was getting "paid." The older pendejas hated la gorda boss,
but Mari covered for her and did her job and shut her mouth. In
exchange, la gorda screamed at everybody but Mari the teenager, who

everybody knew was a teenager, but they didn't know she was only sixteen. Did it matter? No. Mari was invisible when she wanted to be, and that's the way she liked it.

Only one small yellowy bulb floated above the backdoor over Mari's head, a piss-colored light to go with the piss-stink in the alley, and the car-honks from the expressway. From the shadows, 19-year-old Hector showed up, all wiry and muscles and a song in his head as he sway-walked even when no one was looking, he and la Mari locking eyes, and he could tell she was hot for him and he thought, *Maybe tonight*. And even if they didn't do it, he would get satisfied, because la Mari would never leave him just excited, you know, just frustrated, and all engorged, and ready. She had one of those delicious mouths: it didn't take anything from anybody, and it didn't give much away, and that's why it called to whoever saw it, like, "Imagine, those lips on the most tender skin." Ay Mari, how lucky I am, he thought as he kissed her and rubbed his thighs against hers. Mari grabbed his ass under the piss-colored light, and she could feel his thick manhood, what she loved about him, and his smell, this woodsy scent mixed with *sopa* and *carne* and a little sweat from where he worked like a well-mannered slave.

She wanted him to go back to school, to get his GED, just like she was working it in high school in Jamaica, Queens, and getting decent grades despite her job: to have everything, you know? A fly boyfriend who kept her happy, who was sweet to her, education for both of them, and yes, she would let him have her, all of her, soon, maybe tonight, only the stars would know. But that's how she could escape her familia, and how she could escape returning to Narcolandia, and being deported: with her American *Puertorriqueño*, whom she adored, but needed to shape to become, to become… And in Nueva York, her counselors had told her, she could do college at CUNY, undocumented and all, she could keep going, 'cause NYC loved immigrants. Hector loved her too, he loved his mexicana, god what a nice ass she had, and yes he respected her, never cheating on her (the first one ever!), loved how she was so *cariñosa* to him, unlike so many Nuyorican bitches who just sassed his ass, and preferred white boys with money, or black guys who could kill you. El Hector thought there was something about his Maribel, whether it was her *mexicanidad*, or being brought up in a little village near Puebla, but he knew he would do for her what he had never done for any girlfriend, when she asked him—she *had* to ask him, he wouldn't volunteer it, but he would do it—when she dared. Know what I mean? To *give* and make her happy. Hector and Maribel wanted each other hard. Wanted in the way that hurts and also satisfies. Wanted in the way dreams are made of. Even dreams under a piss-colored light, 'cause everybody dreams, just not everybody pays attention to all dreamers.

They stumbled through the backdoor of the Super 8, la Mari already yanking up her blouse from her jeans, and it was three a.m., and Hector kissed her neck from behind as she half-squealed and arched her neck toward her lover, forgetting to lock the door. Nobody was at the motel but the stoner front clerk, and he was usually half-asleep or watching Roger Corman movies, and la gorda was long gone, and only ghosts would show up for their shift before six a.m. when la Mari would be done done for the weekend. Half the Super 8 was empty. Plenty of rooms. Warrens of privacy. More than enough time to clean up a mess for love. Mari left her cleaning cart with her supplies and keys in front of their door. No one would bother them.

Hector, *mi precioso*, she said. You enrolled, right? You turned in the form, right? It's free, it's the library, Hector… She trailed off as he was already sucking her brown tit and cupping the other one, and Maribel moaning, but still possessed of her senses, 'cause la Mari was one of those Latinas who was passion and fire and screams untethered to this or any world, but also pride and earth, also a *caraja* self-possessed. A dangerous Latina no one could or would own, unless, unless…

Yes, *mami*, yes, Hector half-said mid-breath. Turned them in. I'm in composition and geometry. My first two requirements. *Dios mio*, take off your jeans. *Dios mio*, you're so fuckin' gorgeous, Mari. She grabbed his cock and massaged it through his underwear as the head popped out, escaping, seeking her, her emergency-red fingernails so delicate against the thin white fabric, the shiny skin so smooth, the color of *caramelo* in this half-light. Rub me right there, just like that, Mari said softly in his ear, rub there, *precioso*. Not too hard, just like that. Oh, my god, oh my god. Just exactly like that, right there, just so slowly Hector. *Ay, ay, ay*, oh my god, just slowly, in slow circles, oh my god, just there, not too much pressure. *Ay, ay,* just keep going, *precioso*. You, you…are getting me so wet… No…the underwear stays on, for now. The underwear…stays on, *precioso*.

I love you, Mari, he gasped, her brown skin inches from his mouth, yet still melded with his mouth, a breach with no space in between. I love you, Mari. He out of breath, excitement and asthma all rolled into one. The boy was lean and ripped, but he also had this sweetness and vulnerability that attracted her. Not a straight macho. A man, yes, but not a *pendejo* macho like her father's friends. Not a narco macho, not an I'm-gonna-beat-the-shit-out-of-you macho, not an idiot macho. Hector, me too, she whispered, licking his hard brown nipples. Love everything about you. I'll take care of you, *precioso*. Tonight. But I don't want you to just fuck me. You will, *precioso*. Next time. You will. I have condoms anyway, in case, in case, tonight... *Ay, ay, ay*! My dear god, you are so good. Let me just take care of you. Let me just love you... right now. Let me show you, Hector, let me show you everything. Hector's head pushed against the pillows in the darkness, and he found and lost the window's highway half-light, and the room spun as her lips and her tongue touched him in secret places. Did he imagine a dark head for a split second at the window? Where did she learn this? Did she just know how to do this? Chuy, María, y Pepino! Her mouth, she had him, these little bites, oh my god, she had him, and he loved when she had him so splayed, when she could do anything to him, and he ached for la Maribel to do everything, to take control, but her puffs and licks, oh my god, these lightning shocks through his body, fireworks in his mind, supernovas in the ether of this murk, his heart, it felt as if she was whispering on the hairs of his heart, and he loved her like no other woman he had ever met. Hector would do anything for Maribel: she would have to ask, but he would do it, gladly, and he would listen to her for whatever she wanted, how she wanted it, as wet as wet could be, and he would make her as happy as he was at this moment, oh my god. Oh, my dear Xochiquetzal!

The door opposite to heaven burst open, and the piss-colored light flooded the room.

What the fuck? Get the hell out of this room, man! Hector yelled.

What? You? What the hell are you doing here? What the hell!

Both of you *putos*, get your clothes on. Get dressed.

Get the hell out of here! What the hell is wrong with you, bro? You know this guy? Maribel? Fuck.

Julio. His name is Julio. A friend of my father's. Please get out of here!

Friend, *pinche puta*? I'm your uncle, *cabróna*. And you, *güey*, she's already fucked me, *pendejo*. She's already pregnant.

You're a liar! What's wrong with you? You're a fuckin' liar. Don't listen to him, Hector. He's my fuckin' *tío*, but I hate him. Get the hell out of here!

Is that how you talk to your elders? Your father's brother? Your blood?

Fuck you! I kissed him, Hector. I kissed him once and that's it. He wanted me to fuck him and I said no. Fuck you and your lies! Pervert!

So Hec-tor—your name, right?—she fucked me, and right here too. Right on this bed too. She fucks all her hombres here. Dozens of them. *Pinche puta*.

He's lying! Julio, uncle Julio, just, just…stop! You know it's a lie. I haven't been with anybody, Hector. Not that way. Please don't listen to him. I haven't. I kissed him and he grabbed me, and I didn't know, I just wanted to see what it was like. That's it! Months ago! Then he started calling my cell and trying to meet me after school. He started showing up at my father's house, like suddenly, when he wasn't there. I never let him in. I never answered the door. Get the hell out of here! Just leave me alone…

A knife was in Julio's hand, and the hand wasn't trembling, but steady, floating in the darkness, dancing in and out of the piss-colored light floating through the window.

Get your fuckin' clothes on, *hijos de la chingada*! Now!

Uncle Julio, please, please…just leave. I don't want you. I made a mistake. Hector, look at me, Hector, please look at me. I just kissed him. I kissed him and he's pissed 'cause I didn't want him. This was before I met you, Hector. Okay? Months before I met you. I love you, Hector. Not him. Fuck him! I don't know what's wrong with him.

You love this pinche *Puertorriqueño*? This *basura*? This nada?

You, like, fucked up, man? Walk out this door before someone gets hurt.

Hector, I love you. Don't believe a word he says! Uncle Julio, we're not in Mexico! Leave us alone. What's wrong with you? I-don't-want-you.

You insulting me, *puta*? You insulting me again?

I'll tell my father. I'll tell him what you're doing. I'll tell him everything!

He knows, little girl. He knows. Told me to take a knife to both of you. We drank a few tonight and he told me to kill you if I want.

You're lying!

This is so fucked up, man. We're walking out. Maribel, get behind me. We're walking out, old man. We're walking out one way or another.

El Hector had pulled his shirt on backwards, the tag under his chin. La Mari, behind, held his hips as they took a step closer to the door. Julio, *el chato*, this muscular short Olmec-man, appeared like a gargoyle in this light, the hand of the *obrero* half-heartedly slashing the air in front of him, blocking the door. Julio's face—what was it?—smiling, grimacing, or just flushed maroon with too many beers? In and out of the light, almost dancing, the thick hand with the knife slashing the darkness. This, this was what Hector saw, or thought he saw, perhaps *un borracho*, an old man half out of his mind, and this, this was why he lunged for the hand with the knife. La Mari screamed.

The men struggled as Mari tried to make out what was happening, who had what in this murk, a bedroom inside a shipwreck at the bottom of the sea. A deep groan and what sounded like a hiss, and Hector's white shirt, the backwards shirt, soaked red, a side wound. Mari grabbed Julio by the head as he staggered-stumbled onto Hector, and Julio elbowed her in the face with his powerful arm whipping through the air in the darkness, sending her crashing into the bedframe. Hector still fighting, even as Julio groped for the knife, which had clanged somewhere on the floor, Hector yelling, *Motherfucker! You goddamn motherfucker!* El Hector coughing, spitting blood, punching the air, hitting Julio in the balls, and miraculously his ass touched the knife, he's half-sitting on the blade. With his boxer-like arm reaching back and coming forward in a swoosh, Hector stabbed at the figure doubled-over, still half on him, kneeing and punching him, the blade penetrating a neck, Julio's neck. Hector felt a gust of beer breath. Julio screamed a sickening high-pitched wail that would've instantaneously lit the room hospital-fluorescent white if it were light, and vomited. Blood gushing from his neck, Julio collapsed with a thud against the cement floor, writhing, kicking Hector, but just kicking wildly without aim, a rivulet of blood pouring forth from his wound. Gurgling sounds, like perhaps what a small lava pit might sound like in the dark.

In the struggle, the door had been shoved closed. Fucking motherfucker! Mari! Fuck! I think I killed the asshole. Mari! I'm bleeding. It's bad. I can't see. Mari. My hands are wet. I can't stop it! Mari, where the fuck are you?

Only the piss-colored light shimmered through the window. The door was closed. The kicking man, Julio the Olmec, Julio the drunken idiot, Julio stacker of Fairway almonds and walnuts and wasabi peas, Julio easily replaced by another Julio, or José, or Ricardo, Julio soon-to-be-forgotten by even the well-meaning and well-to-do of the Upper Westside, Julio in America, this Julio newly dead. Oh, fuck!

Mari, Hector called out into the darkness, more anguished now, as the blood still coursed through his fingers, lightheaded. Mari. One of the last things he remembered, but not the last thing, was the wetness of the earth, the puddles over him and around him. His blood became their blood.

Hector reached Mari at the other end of the room, next to a spot of light on the floor. Dragged himself a few feet, as his head felt like a balloon filling with helium. The life pouring out of him. He touched her neck in the darkness, he squinting his eyes, trying to catch her face. La Mari. Wake up, Mari, he whispered. Mari, I need your help… The neck twisted at a weird angle. That's what he remembered last. Her neck. How he had kissed it moments before, in a dream. This neck how no neck was ever meant to be.

At six a.m., Esmeralda found the bloody triptych. Esmerelda, *unas de las viejas* who had been cleaning rooms for American citizens for two decades, here at the Super 8 Jamaica North Conduit, but also at many other places across this great land of ours. Julio's car had been idling for hours by the back door.

But before she found them. Before. When no one was there. Before. The three alone under the piss-colored light that still danced through the window, moths hovering for a home, obscuring and revealing the light. All three still. Before humanity discovered what was not human anymore, but what was left. The three in the half-light appeared like fragments of glass splashed with red, a mosaic half-seen and half-unseen in the darkness. It was a perspective from the stars, a perspective before anything, before Esmeralda's screams. Red glass shattered to hint at figures bathed in a yellowy light. The stained glass of another world in a church without a savior, in a church without a purpose.

TURNAROUND IN THE DARK

Eat those Mesopotamian roaches, *pinche* mantis; eat them and disappear into the sand again. Don't bother me in my sleep. That's right, crawl under Levin's boots. Crawl *into* Levin's boots. That'll surprise the bloodsucker tomorrow. I don't know how that animal sleeps through the dust storms. This trailer-can's about to fly away into the night.

What is wrong with my leg? Hey, leg, stop jumping. Can't write. Can't get the words just right, for Lori. This crappy leg is like a piston, with this crate for a desk, and dust in my nostrils and lungs—God, I can't breathe. I'm swimming in this dust. Can't inhale, and Levin's sleeping like a baby. How can he sleep tonight? Maybe I should shove this Bic up his ass, see if that wakes him up. Bouncing leg, pump the right words out for Lori, words of honey mixed with chile. Just keep bouncing, leg, see if that helps. Need the right words. That's what matters, isn't it? Goddamn you, leg. Goddamn everything.

Martinez, Martinez, Martinez, why are you here? Why aren't you in El Paso? Why aren't you sipping a cup of coffee in the teachers' lounge at Americas High, waiting for them to kiss your ass? Staring at the little glories in tight jeans in the hallways—God, some of the seniors must be incredible lays. What I would give to be back there again. What I would give not to be the *culo* principal, but a teenager in Ysleta again, my ass after those little glories. Getting old is shit, and getting old in Iraqi-fucking-stan is worse than shit. Martinez, don't be so hard on yourself. You can still run three miles in less than fifteen minutes, goddamnit. You're an Army lieutenant, Martinez. Act like one. No, really, you're in the Army Reserve, with the older yahoo idiots. You are an older yahoo idiot. But yeah, you're in the Army. And you can still make la Lori scream with dee-light. You can still pop that blond beauty, her eyes rolling, her breath gasping. Everybody's proud of you, Martinez. Chin up, goddamnit! Get your chin the hell up, and stop your old leg before the crate tips over.

God, it's so late. Why am I not asleep? *Tonto* Martinez, you don't have guts. That's why you're here. The glories run your dick. Always. You didn't want to volunteer for another tour, you said so yourself, you didn't want to. You promised yourself you would get out, but what does that matter anymore, right? Why does anything? You had the Army's letter in your hand, you had a choice—at that moment you had a choice, you stupid bastard. And what did you do? Lori squeezed you from behind at exactly the wrong second and squeaked in that sickly sweet voice, "What's that, honey?" You stared into her eyes, with an instant hard-on. After she read the letter, you fired like an M-16, "I'm doing it again." Just the opposite of what you had been thinking. Just the goddamn opposite! What were you thinking, Martinez? Were you even thinking? You fucked her then and there. You picked her up, carried her to your bed, and fucked la Lori for two hours. The hell with your decision and the world that afternoon. And Lori was yours, has always been yours, as yours as anyone can be. But why, you idiot? Would she have cared one way or the other? Did you even stop to think about what you were saying? And why didn't you just take it back? Why didn't you say, "I thought about it without my dick erect, and I'm done with this goddamn Army." Would she have cared? Would anyone have stopped you? Would anyone have said to your face you hadn't been a man? You are a man, moron. You're trapped, Martinez, that's your problem. You're trapped in yourself, ghosts and Al-Que-se-qaeda in your head. But, god, your Lori was and still is an incredible lay. And now you want to go destroy that too. Glories run your dick, that's your problem. They run your dick to the sunny side, the dark side, and back. Let's do it, and be done with it. Who cares why anymore. Write, goddamnit.

I don't know when I'll come back. Can't wait to show this artwork from the kids to Levin. He'll get a kick out of it. That man can't find north from south in this desert after his girlfriend ditched him for his best friend from high school. Stone cold, man. Look at this little soldier-man, with the flag next to him, green hair. Do these kids from Americas Middle School think we're Martians? They're kids, *tonto*, give 'em a break. Lori's got some money now. At least Americas gave her a job. I'm sending her every goddamn penny. Hey, look! Here's Noah's and Sarah's! Knew la Lori would also send drawings from *mis niños*! That's us, all four of us. In Ysleta. The house with the palm tree, that big ol' yellow sun as big as half the sheet of construction paper. Man, I remember that Crayola smell from South Loop School. I bet Pancho and Isela are helping Lori with the kids whenever she's grading papers. They've got to.

I thought about not telling you at all, but then every time I stared at your pictures, at your blue eyes that trusted and believed in me, I felt so guilty. Did that soldier just smile and wink at me? Did she? What an incredible ass. Into the mess tent, Martinez. Go find her, goddamnit. Even if you've already eaten, man. There she is. There she is, with that smile from heaven. Oh, and those delicious tits. Thank you, dear Lord, for saving me from this hell.

Jenna, you sweet and incredible fuck. Jenna, you dream. You're this soldier's dream. A *chingona* with a six pack. A Latina Victoria Secret's model in Iraqi-fucking-stan, and in my tent. In her tent. In the supply room. In the desert at night. In between our trucks. In in in. She screams her muffled screams. She can't have enough of me, I can't have enough of her. I don't care, I don't care, I don't care. If this will save me, I don't care. I want to lick her sweat more than anything else I've wanted in my life. *I ended it, because I know you didn't deserve my betrayal. I ended it, because I couldn't live with myself anymore.*

I was lonely. I was bitter about being here again. I felt trapped. Man, it's goddamn boring in this desert. It's boring, but I have Jenna. It's nothing, it's patrols, it's preparing for another run, but I have Jenna. Yes, Ysleta too, yes home, but faraway. But not now. Right now I have to survive this heat in la nada, these assignments, whenever they come, wherever they go. Right now I have to squeeze Jenna's hips, whisper to her about our plans, convince her of what we'll do when we get home—right?—and yes, fuck her. That's what she wants. That's what I want. What promises have we made to each other? She knows. Does it really matter? I have a reason for being here. She has a reason. That's all that matters today.

I know you will hate me. I know you will think I was weak and stupid and worse. I love you, Lori, and that's God's truth. Jesus H! I can't believe what la Jenna does to me. I can't believe what she lets me do to her. This woman is my woman. I give her every ounce of my self in this hot, hanging night air. When I haven't seen her, when it's been days, my God, we're so hungry for each other. Last night, in that supply truck, I mean, it was rumbling. Thought the damn engine would spontaneously start in our heavenly oblivion. I couldn't breathe in that night heat. She was hyperventilating. Both of us more drained than after any six-mile hike in Iraqi-fucking-stan.

Yesterday I tried to imagine how I would feel if you had told me you had been with another man… I tortured myself, to make me feel how you would feel, to feel that hurt I know I have done to you. She'll like it, la Jenna. She'll love this picture of me. Back home in front of my palm tree. Who cares who was next to me? Now with my scissors, it's a new picture. Just like that. It's me in El Paso. Jenna will remember me when she returns to Kansas City. I'll be home too. One of these days.

You know, the world is safe. It's a lie, and it's not, it's a lie, and it's not. You try to hang on, you try to make it… I know I've hurt you and I'm so sorry. If you forgive me, Lori, and I pray that you do, you will save me.

Have to drop this letter with the mail clerk before we start our mission. I've got about an hour. What idiot in the Army thought of this "Four"? Sacks hanging on a wall? This dopey moron moving packages from one corner to another? That's Camp Fallujah for you. Okay, Martinez, you idiot, why did you walk out? *Why* did you walk out? Drop the goddamn letter in the right bag, and get your job done. What the hell is wrong with you? Lori doesn't deserve it? Is that why? You even know why anymore? You don't deserve it, Jenna doesn't deserve it. What does "deserve" have to do with anything? You just trying to hurt somebody? Is that the sick fuck you've become? Martinez, you even know what you're doing, or why? This moron again. What are you staring at, maggot? I can goddamn stand here and go in and out of this "Four" all day, corporal. Don't give me your "What the fuck?" look, you bastard. I don't need to explain myself to anybody. That's right. Keep walking before I put my boot up your ass. Dumb-ass farm boy, happy to be in the shit. The hell with this happiness. The hell with the mail. I'll do it later, and leave it right here in my shirt pocket. I'll do it when I do it, or I won't and then I won't. This back and forth has got me by the balls. Know your mind, Martinez. Get back and check the gear and see if the men are ready. Get your head on straight.

Where the hell are we? We've been driving for hours. Camp Fallujah to the first checkpoint, a Listening Post, Observation Post. Resupplied. Job done. But where is this second motherfucking LPOP? How hard can it be? Mayhew's driving too fast, but he hasn't lost the other trucks behind us. We can't see shit through this darkness and sand. "It's a secondary road between Fallujah and Baghdad, sir." Why do they have six soldiers guarding the road? Is our company that close to the ragheads in Baghdad North? Our flank, our supply line. Where the fuck are they? No messages on the Blue Force Tracker. The GPS says we're on the right road. "Keep going, Mayhew. We still have to get to our guys outside of Baghdad." Our supply line. These ammo pallets. On the way back, we'll have to find that second motherfucking LPOP.

This goddamn Iraqi desert, what a nightmare! The winds shake these trucks like toys. The Night Vision Goggles are useless in these dust storms. Mayhew, Jesus! He can't see shit in front of him. Nothing but a wall of dust going in and out. Jerky bastard, he looks like a chicken sticking his head out the window. Can he see the edge of the road? This is so fucked up. The road's here, and not here. We're driving blind and I'm in the front seat. The Seven-Bravo NVG's don't give you any depth perception. Why did they waste money on these? The tanker trucks and security Humvees are still behind us, thank God. I don't see the rest, but they must be there. Wouldn't be the first time we lost a truck, or had somebody take the wrong turn. Another night of *desmadres* in one thousand and one nights of *desmadres*. But you know, we've always found our way. We've always found our guys, even if we lost them for a few hours. Last month, that was a scene. A lost gas truck stumbled on an LPOP, unannounced, and the motherfuckers shot out the tires of their own guys. What's better, to be killed by ragheads or friendlies? You're dead. But my platoon always makes it back. We're gonna make it back tonight too. My platoon's always been lucky, Martinez, don't you forget it.

This is the road to nowhere. Where is that second LPOP? Is this even a fucking road? We should have reached the company outside of Baghdad eleven miles east of the second LPOP. I don't see a single sign of the goddamn company. Where the hell are we? Don't hear anything from our last truck. Are they even still with us? Jesus H. Christ! This wind! Did our truck just tilt? I think it's getting worse, if that's possible. A giant Jesus throwing fistfuls of sand at our windshields. Sand in my goggles, sand inside my uniform, sand around my eyelids, sand at the back of my throat, sand up my crack, for God's sake. The windows are shut too. This evil brown talcum powder, not like El Paso's grainy brown dirt. Listen to that. His eyes glued to the road, Mayhew doesn't ever listen to shit. That's the engine whining. The sand's getting into the engine. Won't be long before this clunker dies on us tonight in the middle of nowhere. But Joey can fix anything. That's exactly why he's here. Joey will get it going again, just long enough to get us home.

Answer, goddamnit! Where the hell is this second LPOP, and why don't they answer? What the hell was that pop? Oh, yeah. Can't believe these jerks. Who is doing that? Somebody in the third or fourth truck behind us? I mean, seriously, flinging goddamn fragmentation grenades out the window? Told these morons not to do that anymore. Told them, but maybe I should just bust their ass like Lieutenant Levin. Then maybe they'll listen. Maybe I should force these yahoos to clean toilets for three days, see if that doesn't wake them up. Don't be weak, Martinez! But this is what happens. They're nervous as shit— who the hell *is* that?—and they start with their stupidity. But we've never lost a single soldier. Never been nailed by a Rocket-Propelled Grenade. Not a single casualty. And what are we doing now? Fighting the dust with fragmentation bombs. Fighting the fear. The enemy's always waiting for us, behind the dust cloud, deciding to strike when it pleases them. Why fight us straight up? Why fight us when we're ready? They know better. A goat herder not blinking his eyes as we go by his concrete hut on the dusty banks of an irrigation canal. That hard silence in his eyes. "Why don't you get the fuck out of my country?" Is he imagining what's around the bend for us? An RPG screeching at us like a motherfucking Dementor? Where the hell are we, and how did we miss that second LPOP?

Martinez, Martinez, Martinez, what has happened to you in Iraq? Three years ago, your men saluted you for the first time, and what did you see? All of them jittery, jerky bastards. Couldn't keep their eyes in one place. You thought it was like a disease, like an itchy disease you get in the desert. Iraqi gonorrhea. One month later, your ass is deep in that itchy Iraqi disease. "Where's it coming from? Who's around that corner?" Those questions like bees inside your brain, even inside Camp Fallujah. Some people, that farm boy at the post office, it's like they're on vacation. Still grinning. Not thinking. But that's what you have to do. Stop thinking. Martinez, that farm boy's smarter than you. Can you self-lobotomize? But how can you even trust the Moroccans and Somalis spooning out the chow? How can you trust these Iraqi policemen who don't want you there, who are so goddamn incompetent? For a few dollars and for their hatred of the "ulooj," the American infidel pigs, those Iraqi shits will sell your ass to hell in the Green Zone.

Martinez, you've become the landscape. Home, hah! You go back to El Paso between deployments, and you notice it. You talk faster than you did. You can't keep your focus, your eyes skip across the landscape with the Iraqi itch, from Lori's blue eyes to the window, ready for something to happen. And she asks you, "Honey, why are you awake? What's wrong?" Every "honey" makes you want to scream and pummel her face, but you say nothing. The front door's rattle freaks you out, for no reason. You can't say anything. It's imagination, it's history. Everything and nothing. You won't tell her that. It's shots being fired at you through the dark as you speed by a hamlet engulfed by dust. It's a soldier carried back from the lines, his left shoulder and arm smoldering. An Improvised Explosive Device nailing a Humvee. Or strange, unaccountable explosions in the distance as you nod off in the Green Zone. It's stories that aren't stories, but accounts from men a few miles from where you are now. This bleak and foreign land you're trapped in. The wary looks of entire families as your platoon drives by. What primal, inscrutable message are they burning into your brain with their eyes? What message you sending them? Who would ever understand? Eyes on the road, goddamit!

Stop day dreamin'! Where's your brain, Martinez? Your brain is in Iraq even when your body is in Ysleta, or Kansas City. These days in the desert, like years. These days waiting for nothing to happen, until something does. Your brain on adrenaline, hyped-up, bored beyond boredom, yet still coiled like a Texas rattlesnake. What's happened to you, goddamnit? Seven months in Iraq, seven scars in your brain. Didn't you get back home? You were back home, you idiot, but then they called you up again. You should've learned your lesson, you should have been a man when you needed to be a man. You shouldn't have let these little glories run your ass back to Iraq. You should've done it to save your ass, to get rid of these nerves once and for all. You should've done it to be done with this godforsaken land. But you chose to be a jittery, jerky bastard.

Martinez, mail this fucking letter in your pocket. Mail it before it burns a hole straight to your heart. Tonight, yes tonight, you will be able to promise her anything. Tonight you can fuck Jenna in her tent until morning. You can tell her you told Lori. You can lie and tell the truth and lie again and pray something happens. Anything. Return. You'll be free for a few days after this mission.

"Holy shit. We're on the wrong road. Just got a text from our first LPOP. We've got to turn around, get everybody turned around. They say we're probably on a side road that's unmarked, a fucking farm road, I think."

"Hey, listen up! The lieutenant says we're turning the fuck around! Right here! So keep your fucking eyes opened!"

Okay, get everybody moving. We're moving. We're not waiting in the dark like targets in a shooting gallery. Okay, we're fine. First LPOP, finally, somebody responds. What the hell is their problem? We're returning after we took the wrong turn. West. We need to head west and find that turnoff we missed. Finally we can see in front of us. The wind and sand at our backs, and not in our faces. Jesus, what a crazy night. The dust storms seem to have died down. God, I can see it now. Mayhew sees it too. We've been on a road, not much of a road, next to an irrigation canal. We're on a dirt road next to what looks like a levee. Smaller canals breaking off from the main canal, toward—what?— fields or farms. It's like one of those old flickering movies. Curtains of dust appearing and disappearing, giving you a peek at the landscape and then just as quickly yanking it away. You think you see it, and your mind makes up the rest. A spinning that's going forward. These NVG's, they're useless.

We're okay after that turnaround in the dark.

What the fuck? What just happened? An explosion. Did the engine explode? Blue lights and flashes of fire. We're on the side. Are we on the side? What just happened? Are we tumbling down a canal? The truck, my God, I think we're hit. I can't breathe. From the windshield, a sea of sand pouring in. I can't breathe. I'm drowning in sand. Why is there glass on my chest? These NVG's on my nose?

God, my neck. What's wrong with my neck? Is it glass? Shrapnel? A warm trickle above my left knee. I can't move my legs. What happened to my goddamn legs? I can't move my body. Have I lost my legs? Can't see very well. Yes, my legs. Who's shouting? Blurry red in front of me, my God, that must be a fire. This milky red a few feet in front of me, but no heat. Can't feel the heat. My head, I can't… What? Thump-thump-thump, my boys with their M-16's. "We got the motherfuckers! We got them!" Mayhew, what happened to him? If I can turn, if I can just push myself… Oh, God. Donny. Donny. There's not much left of you. God. Al Jarreau, Donny. Won't forget you taught me about Al Jarreau. God. It must've hit on Donny's side, whatever the fuck hit us. My waist. Am I peeing in my pants? What's wrong with my waist and back? A hand yanking my uniform. What the…? Chunks of flesh on my chest, fuck. They're trying to yank me out the window, these motherfuckers. My head, in blue water. Everything blue.

Noah and Sarah, my babies. In the canal behind our house in Ysleta. My brothers Pancho and Mayello, and Julieta, all of us hiding too in the canal. Burning tumbleweeds. Laughing. A voice from behind the rock wall on San Lorenzo Avenue. My mother Pilar, her voice in the wind. Corporal Johnson. Why the hell are you here? What you doing in Ysleta? Jenna, oh Jenna, your brown eyes in ecstasy. Your eyes have always wanted me. Those eyes, my eyes. No pain. It's gone. Only this twisting cloud. A bluish cloud of dust in the night. Are we in Ysleta? Where are we? Nothing but more words in the wind.

ALONE TOGETHER

I didn't find a current photo of my old girlfriend on the Internet, but I did find the upper body selfie of her daughter at a college in Cali. Her face in mid-laugh reminding me so much of her mother Melissa I surprised myself with my heart racing. Long before this middle age, we had been one in Boston, Melissa and me, and now this young thing in front of my eyes, a genetic echo of the mother in the daughter. How long ago was it since I delivered myself so unwillingly? On Manhattan's Upper Westside, how many women in black yoga pants sauntered by me, and I, well, only with my memories? The daughter Gina, this pixie, so sleek and whimsical, with the delicate curves her mother possessed in her twenties, the same long, smooth legs and wide hips. Thirty years ago, that easy, adventurous smile was the jewel that saved me from a post-college cubicle-prison. Her vulnerability, too. We were young. We were ravenous for each other. Now in my mind, I remembered the young Melissa, across the electrons on the screen, across a wishful wormhole of time. Years ago, for hours and hours, I lost myself in reveries with her. But is there ever a return to the past? Can the past ever return to the present? Is a circle perfect, or just a perfect echo? A man can fail, and does indeed fail: it's one of the sorriest sights of all.

The mind changes and stays the same, the heart changes and stays the same.

I discovered that Melissa married Donald, the dweeb, and that old Don achieved lawyerdom outside of LA. Melissa would have made love to me all the way to California, if I had stayed with her, even if I had never lived in California and never wanted to. Who would ever prefer Cali over Nueva York, Manhattan, even Brooklyn? Zombies, stoners, mid-western wannabes. Melissa never stopped yammering about California and about her Chinese mother warning her against Mexicans, against *me*. Yet who rocketed her little girl to shrieks of delight in the Back Bay? Nobody I ever made love to had been a songstress like Melissa. As we made love to each other, Meli-girl moaned this shocking, deep walrus moan. I always wondered, Am I…is that…*me*…*her*? She lost herself in me, her eyes rolled back to a white nowhere. She gave herself to me, in a way only a woman could. I exploded like a dying red star. It was always the sweetest of deaths. I coaxed Melissa and brought her to her drama explosions. She in turn bequeathed to me that precious gift of becoming stardust for a few seconds. Is that why I have never forgotten her? For entire afternoons I was with her—and on Sunday mornings—until the two of us fused into one. Donald never won that part of her soul. Donald was putting la Meli *la la*. Donald was Japanese. After work, Melissa always invited me to her place, whenever library Don was lost in law school exams. I was with Charlotte then. I still am, in a way. Melissa and I had been fugitives. But from what, really?

On Zillow I also found what Melissa and Donald paid for their house in Santa Monica. The Duck must have made a pretty good living. He must have nailed it, moola-wise, 'cause I couldn't find Melissa on Google anywhere, maiden name or married name, except for modest donations to private schools, and their attendance at a parents' weekend at a small college by the Pacific Ocean. Always Melissa listed her maiden name: Melissa Sun. No doubt she was *la jefa* in their little palace-by-the-sea, even if she only took care of Gina and her boy Bruce. Yeah, the kid Bruce gave it all up on his Facebook page and bought too many video games—that's how I found my first real clues about my long-lost Melissa. Indeed, without the son I would have never found the mother. Kids are always the weak links when you seek anonymity on the Internet. At least their house was not more expensive than mine, and I had done well too, but wouldn't it be nice to see old Meli in a shack, divorced, fat? Wouldn't it be a kind of victory to know she would've been better off with me? I know she would've been happy. I would've treated her like a precious *reina*. But who made that choice? I could've easily said yes. I could've said yes when I had to. I could've been with Meli all these decades, if I had uttered the right words next to the Mormon fountain in the Back Bay. If I had grown some balls in Connecticut. If I appreciated my mistakes before it was too late to change my paths to the future. I had my chances. I have only myself to blame.

I imagined that Meli was sleeping with the Duck out of gratitude for taking care of her, because, yes, she wanted to be taken care of. She had her own mind, yet she loved when someone just took her. I remembered Meli chatting with me at my first job, with the biggest of smiles, she leaning against my cubicle desk and touching my arm, always inviting *herself* and talking my ear off about Bruce Springsteen.

Back in the day, the Boss was it in Boston. I remembered her wearing those orange-and-yellow sundresses with spaghetti straps slipping off her thin brown shoulders. That short black hair. I thought about that smooth as silk skin every day. I wanted Meli's fragility in my hands. I remembered her laughing, her mouth in a gigantic O, and how she would linger at my desk as I was computing who-knows-what-the-heck-anymore, how she would touch my forearm right before she returned to her desk. The atmosphere of that deathtrap crackled like the red gas next to the lip of a volcano, my young heart aching for la Meli. Every part of my will stopped me from touching and holding her hands, pulling her closer to whiff her perfume on my Herman Miller ergonomic. She loved to get close to me. I think she knew she was torturing me. And yeah, I eventually asked her if she wanted to come up to my apartment and listen to "The River," and I loved her in a symphony of walrus moans. In the Back Bay. In my dingy apartment overlooking the Fens. On swivel chairs and sofas. On shag carpets and hardwood floors. We even devoured each other on her mattress on the floor in her apartment, because, yeah, that's what it felt like, to eat and be eaten. When she came, when she gasped in the dark in her death throes, she squeezed me uncannily, as if gripping my entire body would save us. But, of course, that's not how she had me. That's not how I had her. For afternoon after afternoon, we were alone together.

I tried to remember that day in Connecticut. This, as a few weeks later, I noticed Meli and the Duck were knee-deep in California property taxes. I found, hah! A client review of lawyers. Here's the Duck: "If I could give a negative number to this lawyer I would. He showed little passion for the work he did for me (unsuccessful), and seemed distracted." You said it, sister. That's what you get Meli-my-issa, for choosing the Donald. A passionless, distracted Duck. Surely in their bed, she's in the arms of Morpheus early. Without question, she's not sweaty and sticky and savage for more at four in the morning. But maybe she's made her peace with it. Would she have been happy with me? Would I have been happy with her? I tried to remember, without prejudice, that day in Connecticut. This history: I wanted to understand.

I had abandoned the Boston version of Kafka's prison. I had not told Meli-girl, or Charlotte—whom I was still seeing on the sly—that Marilyn had tried too. Marilyn my boss, Marilyn Meli's boss, Marilyn an econometric genius. Back then I thought Marilyn, just short of forty, was old, and now I'm a decade older. The boss had invited me to her condo after work for a drink. Hers an old-world apartment just off the Boston Commons, with a little garden. I was astonished by the garden, and I realized Marilyn must've made serious money as an economist. Who had a garden a few feet from Faneuil Hall? Well, Marilyn. She also was the most gorgeous economist I had ever met, with the smoldering intensity of a Lauren Bacall. I was twenty-three, and twenty pounds lighter, and out of my league. After a few drinks, as I stood admiring her little paradise in the middle of Bean Town skyscrapers, Marilyn pressed against me and kissed me delicately on the lips so surprisingly, I stumbled back into a bookshelf and smacked my spine against a sharp edge! Man, I wanted to be with Marilyn too. But she whispered, after I composed myself and wrapped my arms around her waist and tasted her crimson lips and lovely neck, "What about Charlotte?"

Yeah, my boss knew about my "serious girlfriend," and my boss would've ravaged my young ass in her garden, and all over that condo, had I simply lied and said Charlie-girl was history. I hadn't lied to Meli, and she had been sleeping with me all year. Meli didn't care. Well, Marilyn wasn't like that, Marilyn's was an old-school morality, and yet Marilyn let me kiss her everywhere for a minute or two. My Econo-boss, in a huffy mid-pant, gently guided my face back to her eyes. Marilyn, she seemed from another dimension. An adult's adult. "That's enough. No more for you, horny young Mex," or something more artful from her full lips. The next day, in her white silk blouse and tight black skirt, Marilyn smiled behind her Irish eyes and her giant oak desk. She whispered with the office door closed, "If you change your mind, you know where I am." A few weeks after that, I left for Connecticut, I left because I couldn't stand that Boston air any longer, I left because I was as close as an ant's butt to the ground to changing my mind for real and breaking up with Charlotte. I didn't know what I wanted anymore. Boston was too damn cold for too long. Marilyn and Melissa haunted me at night like a human-headed Orthrus. Even Charlotte. I left to get away from all of them. I left to be my own boss like Marilyn. I left because I didn't want to rot in a cubicle. I left for all those reasons, and none of them. I still don't know why I left…but I did.

Connecticut was trees. Connecticut is trees. I thought I was safe in Connecticut from myself, from them. I was in graduate school. I was, well, eyeing that black French graduate student, with her bottomless-pit hazel eyes and gap-tooth smile, as she sashayed in long skirts down Whitney Avenue. Eve never wore anything but long skirts. Eve laughed when I mentioned regression analysis. But I hadn't kissed

Eve yet. I was clearing my head. I was sleeping on a foam mattress atop plywood on cinderblocks, and thinking about Eve every night. I was a cheap bastard. I still am. I didn't care about money, but I wanted it in the bank, like a pair of delightful blankets to keep me warm at night. I wanted a certain mental freedom, even in my Rockport ProWalkers.

Oddly Eve, or Meli, or Charlotte, even Marilyn—all the same: they also didn't give a rat's ass about money. They did, but they didn't, you know? They didn't care I was a Chicano, or maybe they liked me because I was a Chicano. I never understood why. A Connecticut Chicano in the Court of Queens. Most assume if you love women, if you're sleeping with them, that you're a macho scumbag. If you're sleeping with several of them, then you're Doctor Macho, PhD in Scumbaggery. But these were women who gave me what they wanted to give me. Nothing more. Women who loved me to change me. When they didn't get what-who they wanted, they left. Women with money. Women with plans. Women with other men. Wham, bam, thank you, sir! All but one used and loved me like I used and loved them. I was as much left in a pile of nothing as they were. Someone please study what's action, and what's reaction, because I only know the fog of love.

So I was hanging with Eve in New Haven, not doing anything yet except learning French cuss words, and who showed up one day? La Meli. There she was from Boston, off the Amtrak for a visit, with a picnic basket! I imagined every sandwich was laced with a date drug. I imagined she was trying to trick me, and of course she was. She sat on my foam mattress, her gaze lost in the elm treetops outside my window. Spaghetti strap fell carelessly off her shoulder. I glimpsed

at her breast, because of course she's not wearing a bra. And when
my hand touched her thigh, a crackle of electricity raced through my
fingers. Before I could find the blue sky again, Meli was on top of me.
I made love to her all night, and she made love to me. Meli walrus-
moaned and screamed, a deliciously awful aria that lifted me beyond
the elm treetops at my window. A concert-in-the-clouds for herself and
for me. I imagined the molecules in every brick in that brownstone
trembling with Meli's songs. Later I knew every grad student inside
that Queen Anne had been eavesdropping too. Certainly that blond
from Indiana across the hall of cracked linoleum tiles: only the two
of us on the third floor. The next night, after I had escorted Lincoln-
Center Meli to the train station, the blond—in a white bathrobe—
opened her door just as I fumbled with my door key. She must've heard
my footsteps. Amanda invited me for tea. She a Music Theory grad
student, and yeah, a so-so friend, but without that mesmerizing Song
of the near-Dead.

But old man, you're getting ahead of yourself. Maybe that
bad habit was why I got ahead of myself back then, and failed to
appreciate what happened that weekend with Meli. I was in that fog
of intelligent, uninhibited women. La Meli had arrived with her picnic
basket to ask me if I had told Charlotte. If I had revealed what I could
not yet reveal, if I had declared the two of us as one. Meli had fed me,
loved me all day Saturday, and asked me about Charlotte at three in
the morning. A sweet ambush. I was clueless. That's when, if I had
wanted Melissa, that would've been the moment to say it, to stake my
flag in this new territory, whether I believed it was mine or not. As
soon as I blurted out that I could not hurt Charlotte—what possessed

me to tell the truth?—Meli retorted that she had not told the Duck either. Slapped me with those words to defend herself, to mask the pain in her brown eyes. Both of us wanted the other one to push "us" into a new truth. I understand it now, decades later, but back then I thought it was more of the same—I thought I would just keep loving Meli in New Haven. I imagined I was in control. What a storytelling fool I was! Meli even made love to me again that Sunday afternoon, after the mushroom-onion-sausage pie at Sally's, but now I know it was a farewell fuck. A mercy. I believed I owned Melissa's beautiful song, but really, Meli dearest was just doing me a favor. It has taken decades for me to appreciate this. That is the problem with men. Always beyond late to understand the moments that matter.

I loved Charlotte. I still love Charlotte. If I had to hurt someone in New Haven, I wouldn't hurt Charlotte. Not that I wanted to hurt Melissa. I just couldn't hurt Charlotte, you know? Her blue eyes seemed so sad to me. Char had always been sweet too, although struggling against waves of bitterness and selfishness these last three years. Char wanted me, really loved me, and that's why I loved her. Does that any make sense? That's why I couldn't hurt her. Meli wanted me, yes, she was hungry for me, but was that ever *love*? I was never sure. I didn't know what love was. Perhaps I will never know. Back then I just accepted Charlotte's faith in me. It carried me and saved me, even at the moment when I felt like ending it all on Orange Street.

A few weekends after Meli returned to Boston, Charlotte also arrived on the Amtrak to visit me in New Haven. I was still talking to Melissa, I was still making plans in my foolish head, but now Charlotte was on Orange Street. She chasing after some good guy I knew I wasn't. She, wanting me in a way I've never even wanted myself, or anybody else, for that matter. A certain purity lived in Charlotte's want, and a certain stupidity, because I knew in my rotten heart who I was. Both of us sat on that same foam-plywood-cinderblock bed, Meli's scent still planted deep inside that foam-pore universe. Charlotte stared at me, believed in me, and what did I do? I told her. I told her everything. A prick, that's what I was.

Was it that sweet weakness in her eyes? Or the painted cruelty in my heart? Was I trying to get Charlotte to save me from my wretched self? What a coward. Was I trying to bury myself under the earth, to see myself fight for a breath? If Charlotte had left me, if she had forsaken me, I would have never pulled back from the Helen Hadley Hall ledge that winter. I wanted her to kill me, with my words. I wanted to see her pain. I used her even then, sick son-of-a-bitch that I am. Have I changed after all these years? As it was, Charlotte sobbed in New Haven, sucked her breath deep inside her as if I had flung a pole into her chest. I confessed to Charlotte that I had ended it with Melissa. I lied to save her. I lied to save myself. I told her to *force* myself to be a good man. Yet in my head I almost inadvertently giggled at Charlotte's bleak pain. What kind of depravity that, what kind of *fear*? Perhaps it was dark proof that I would never leave Charlotte. That fear. I am still a sick human being for doing that to her. My older self knows this. Is that the only proof I have ever accepted from anybody? Is that what it takes for me to believe? What the hell has been wrong with me all these years?

I married Charlotte. I married her after five years of "going out," after five years of paper cuts and deep slashes from her parents, who've always hated me because I was not a Jew. Well, now they tolerate me, because I stayed with Charlotte, despite the awful trials. Charlotte was a great mother. We had Sophia and Alexander. I'm as rich as old Marilyn, who's probably dead by now, her remarkable mind and face relished only by worms. I'm another rich economist whose opinion everybody wants, even happy Pomona College next to the Pacific Ocean. Charlotte? Charlotte. She always hated driving, and I'd always driven everywhere, even in Connecticut when we bought our weekend house, for the kids, for us. But Charlotte still drove, in her tentative way, half-frightened. Charlotte didn't know how to take that dangerous turn in the Litchfield hills on Route 202, on her way to buy farm-fresh ice cream at Arethusa Dairy. Charlotte hit a boulder near the shoulder, careened into a tree with the Honda Pilot, and well... It's too much to remember. I remembered hearing the medevac helicopter overhead as I split another stump of wood, and I remembered thinking, "Oh shit, that's close. Wonder what happened." I remembered glancing at the open garage door and realizing Charlotte wasn't back from buying groceries. I remembered seeing the kids in the back, chasing each other with pump-action emergency-orange water guns. I remembered the phone ringing after a while, and me yelling at the kids to get the phone, and stepping out of the shower, dripping wet, pissed off...and my life changing forever.

Yes, I loved Charlotte. I loved that she was still there, even without her leg. I loved that she never felt sorry for herself, that she's never stopped being a great mother to her kids. She was better than me, I know that. I've always known that. Perhaps I knew that instinctually the moment, thirty years ago, when I had stopped myself from telling Melissa I wanted her as much as she wanted me in New Haven. After the accident, I loved that Charlotte took it upon herself to keep me happy in all sorts of ways. I made love to her, even without her leg. It was easier in a way. The small blanket she delicately draped over her stump never failed to slay me. She was trying. And me? I'd never leave Charlotte. She's better than me. But the accident, the years, hurt me too, in a different way than Charlotte. At least she could point to her prosthesis for understanding. What could I point to? What am I missing?

How could Charlotte get a blood clot after her amputation? How was that ever just? A person faces the worse nightmare, she crawls through a dark tunnel and somehow makes it to the other side, bloodied but alive, only to find a gun pointed at her head in the sun. Charlotte, dear Charlotte. It started with a series of infections, which they assured us were a common problem of amputations. The cause? Charlotte's poor blood circulation. Antibiotics. Then a change in her antibiotics. Maybe even Charlotte started to give up by giving end-of-the-world advice to her grown children. We returned to the hospital. I blamed them, for not doing it right the first time. More hospital stays, when "this" would solve it. I was exhausted. More gut-twisting silent nights next to each other. Did God hate me, or just Charlotte? Did God hate me *through* Charlotte? What difference did it make? If He hurt her, He hurt me. Months in a strange fantasyland where I have questioned everything I have done. Months to the end. Every choice I ever made in front of me. This godforsaken ground beneath me. A fistful of dirt stuffed in my mouth. A blood clot in Charlotte's chest. I deserved it. She didn't.

Out of the blue, Pomona College asked me to give a talk on my latest book. I don't believe anything I've written for the past ten years. I don't believe it as if my life depended on it. I don't know what the point is anymore. But I keep writing anyway, to get through each night. I would've ignored Pomona, and anything like Pomona, without thinking about it for a minute. But I vaguely remembered something I came across on the Internet a few months ago. I've always had a heckuva memory. Maybe remembering is my curse. Remembering doesn't necessarily help you today if today is already gone. I remembered someone at Pomona, but it wasn't someone I knew exactly—how could that be? The economists at Pomona, no one I knew, or cared about on their faculty page. I was about to turn Pomona down by Gmail, and then…I remembered.

I instead said yes. I imagined seeing her, Gina, the daughter, who might lead me back to Melissa, the mother. I imagined Gina attending my talk, having a conversation after the lecture, as so many undergrads do to network, to ask fake questions. Maybe I could ask Gina her last name and mention I knew a woman from California, who lived in Boston, who reminded me of her… I imagined not rewriting history, not reliving it, but being at a similar moment in time, the same but different, and what would I do? Memory and imagination, and maybe an escape. I imagined what I thought was a real possibility, not a fantasy. I know things now I did not know then, but did it matter anymore? I was there, but was I too late? At a certain point before the lecture in California, I asked myself, finally understanding and seeing the absurdity at the same time: What the hell am I doing? Why am I here? Memory and imagination, my trap.

After the lecture, I drive toward the fog on Ventura Beach. Why, I don't know. I don't want to return to my hotel room near Pomona College. I have answered their questions. I did my job and ate lunch with those who will likely never do work anyone believes in. I have been polite, even friendly. They care about my work, but I don't—is that really any better? Perhaps it is worse. There was no Gina, of course. There was nobody even remotely resembling Gina or Melissa or Charlotte who could take me back—or forward—in time. What I am is an old man. I have answered all questions. I am so far away from New York City, the only home like a home even when it was barely one. I am an old man alone on a beach in the fog.

I walk into the Pacific Ocean and imagine walking underwater all the way to Hawaii, making more choices, good choices, authentic choices. Underwater, I-am-drowning choices. Perhaps one of these days I will. But what has been lived must be first cleansed away, before one can walk on the sand again. I have to drown me, before I can breathe again. I have to choose someone again, not for who she was, or who she could be, but just for who she is in front of me. And she has to choose me. The moment perfect. After that, you must endure what the earth gives you, all of its passion and bitter roots.

A sand dollar breaks under my foot. The ocean mercifully rinses my blood away.

CROSS-CUTTING RIVERS IN THE SKY

The plane rocks gently on the tarmac, as passengers slowly wend their way through the impossibly narrow aisle to their seats, bumping the headrests flared like small blue wings. Someone gasps behind Melissa, but she does not turn around. She is almost at her seat in 18B as she sees the rain lashing against the plane's windows, in her mind willing everyone to hurry so they can take off from Houston before this flight, too, is cancelled, before she will be stranded half a country away from LA. Which is still four hundred miles from San Francisco. Which is maybe one night away, if Bruce does not get ahold of Gina in time, if Melissa is stranded in El Paso and misses her last connecting flight. Melissa shoves her rollaboard into the overhead bin, drops into her aisle seat and prays someone small, like her, will take the window seat, someone without too much junk, not a teenager, not a fat man or woman, not a man at all, preferably. There is no chance this seat will be empty a week before Christmas. She wants to read, decides to read, and takes out her so-so novel to distract her during the few hours left of this disastrous travel day. One row in front, the little boy across the aisle picks his nose, and the mother settles him into his seat, with singsong sentences in Spanish. Melissa can see him peeking at her through the gaps in the seats, mirth in his eyes. Why hasn't Melissa ever learned Spanish?

"Excuse me. That's my seat."

Melissa smiles and stands up awkwardly, the left big toe still bothering her in the flat black shoes, a strange tingling, as if it were alive and independent of her body like a ligament worm wiggling to escape her flesh. She steps into the aisle. A woman, younger than her—Melissa thinks about ten, fifteen years younger, but usually she guesses wrong and underestimates the age—slips into 18A. Blond. A real blond. In jeans. A youngish mom with a good figure. Pretty. Perhaps quiet. Just the kind of person Melissa may have a pleasant conversation with. Not someone to avoid necessarily for two hours.

Melissa closes her eyes. She decides not to say anything until the plane departs. Maybe never. She hears a crinkling next to her. She doesn't open her eyes. The plane is finally pulling away from the gate. She hears more Spanish. Actually, now that she thinks of it, several Spanish conversations continue around her, one directly behind her. She opens her eyes and notices most souls onboard are Latino, she guesses Mexican-American, but she could be wrong. She's often wrong in San Francisco, but even LA is mostly Chicano. Across the aisle, she sees a man with mutton chops, a cowboy hat on his lap. Others are in cheap plaid shirts with almost maroon skin, like many of the gardeners in her neighborhood. Another behind her wears black, scuffed cowboy boots. Flight 4165 is indeed going to El Paso, Texas. Next to her is one of the few blond persons on the plane. Melissa's hair is black and straight and short, with a few strands of gray. She has always wondered if a few of her Chinese ancestors crossed the Bering Strait, eons ago, to populate North America and Mexico and Guatemala, becoming the Kiowa, Apache, Aztec, and Maya.

She closes her eyes and remembers someone she knew decades ago, right after graduate school in Boston. The last man she slept with before Donald. The last man she slept with after Donald. She married Donald. Melissa hasn't thought of this lover for years: she smiles as she remembers his nickname for Donald. *Quack*. The plane lifts from the ground and rocks from left to right, and this takes her breath away, half in fear and half in wonder. For the next five minutes she thinks about not dying and miracles, and doesn't pray, but hopes to keep going, just to keep moving through the dark clouds, a vessel within a vessel in time.

"You live in El Paso?"

"Yes, returning home. You?"

"No, no. San Francisco. In the north. Presidio Heights. It's been a long, awful day."

"Oh, so sorry to hear that."

"My flight from Boston to San Francisco was cancelled. Couldn't find anything available. The airline offered me this crazy route from Boston to Houston to El Paso to LA. If I can get there, I can probably get a ride with my daughter to San Francisco, if my son has gotten ahold of her. These are the only connections they had available. Snowing in Chicago. Thunderstorms in Houston. Denver's also snowed in. System failures. Bureaucratic chaos. Nothing's available. But this."

"Oh. For me it was just El Paso to Houston and back, to visit my sister. Gotta get back to my kids. Would you like a cracker?" The blond woman unwraps the plastic from a stack of Suzie's Thin Puffed Corn Cakes.

"Thank you. That's very nice of you."

"I have cheddar cheese pieces too." She pinches open a clear plastic baggy with chunks of cheddar irregularly cut.

For some reason, the baggy reminds Melissa of grade school, of her mother in grade school. Her mother who knew Mandarin well. Her mother who's been dead for five years. The taste combination is surprisingly pleasant, and she takes another look at her companion. "So what's El Paso like? I've never been there." Her old lover was from El Paso.

"Well, you'll see when we get closer, when we land. The mountains. These huge mountains right next to downtown. It's the desert too. Very dry. It might get windy this time of year, and at night the temperature drops, and it's cold. But I love it. Where I was born. The sunsets are to die for."

"I'm Melissa Sun, by the way."

"Lori Martinez. Nice to meet you."

"So, isn't El Paso mostly Mexican-American? I mean, are you… but…?"

"My husband was. I'm, I'm…a mutt. Irish, Scottish, maybe a little German. Mostly a mutt. But yes, the city's probably three-quarters Mexican or Hispanic, like my husband, who was born in Texas. His parents are—were from Juárez."

Melissa stops staring at Lori's blue eyes and turns to face the back of the seat inches from her face, thinking she has detected the faintest glistening. "Oh."

"My husband… I'm…I'm a widow."

"Oh, gosh. I am so sorry. You are so young!"

"Thank you. Well, it's been... He was in the military and died in Iraq. It's one of the reasons I visited my sister in Houston. So I could talk to my family. So I could get out a little bit. El Paso's full of soldiers from Fort Bliss. It's still sometimes hard..."

"Oh, I am so sorry."

"I'm fine. It's actually good that I talk about it. Everyone's encouraging me. Hope you don't mind."

"Of course not! I can only imagine. My god." Melissa waits for a moment, before continuing. "So your children are at home?"

"Noah and Sarah, nine and five, yes. They're with my brother-in-law. He and his wife have been great, encouraging me to take some time for myself. Pancho and Isela don't have kids themselves. His family's all in El Paso."

"So you get along with his family?"

"Oh, yes. They've been terrific. Don't know how I would have survived this past year without them. We're having a big Christmas dinner next week at my mother-in-law's house... Marcos. That's my husband. At the house where he was born..."

Melissa notices a tear fall across Lori's cheek and plop onto her lap and soak into her jeans.

"How many kids do you have?" Lori continues.

"Two like you. A boy and a girl, but they're older. Bruce is a senior in high school and Gina's already in college. Pomona. I'm old—oh, my god. I *hate* turbulence." Melissa stares out the window, past Lori's gaze, and only faceless dark clouds flitter across the glass. Nothing to hold onto. She shudders, but at the same time also wills her shoulders still. In the wind, the plane sways in a sickening fashion, the line of sight of the aisle seesawing amid the nothingness underneath them. "Does it ever bother you?" Inside Melissa's stomach, her lingering fear seems to have split her open. Talking seems to help contain this widening rift.

"It does. I try to ignore it. It used to bother me more. But, now, well, it's out of my control... That's how I think about it."

"I worry about—can I ask you a personal question?" Melissa glances forward, and the little boy one row in front is asleep, the top of his brown head just into the aisle, at rest on his mother's lap. If the flight attendants aren't careful, she thinks, the drink cart will hit the little boy's head. *Don't panic*, she repeats inside her head. *Control it.* "You aren't Hispanic. But your husband was. Did it ever matter? You said you get along well with his family."

Lori stares at Melissa for a second too long. Melissa immediately turns away, somewhat ashamed. "It's okay. I've thought about that question, and a million others, this past year. After I got the news from Fallujah. You replay every choice you made in your life. The choices others made." Lori holds her hands together, fingers laced, eerily calm, or pretending to be calm.

The flight attendants are still buckled into their seats. The plane rocks and flutters and hits air pockets that keep launching an invisible ball up Melissa's chest, through her throat. The plane climbs in nauseating bursts. "It's just... A long time ago... Before I was married...I knew someone. Anyway, we were together." Melissa grips the hand rest, and then holds her open palm gently against the seat in front of her. That rift inside her, a chasm.

"He was Hispanic? Mexican?"

"Yes."

"Every family's different." Lori's eyes calmly scan the airplane and stop at the sleepy little boy resting on his mother's lap. Melissa follows Lori's gaze to the boy too. She notices Lori's heartfelt smile. This soothes Melissa.

"I don't mean to pry." Melissa keeps her eyes away from the stormy window, and ignores the awful mutton chops across the aisle and focuses on Lori's sky-blue eyes. Serene, they seem serene.

"Marcos's family treated me—*treats* me—like I'm a part of them. Marcos's mother, Pilar, at the funeral, almost a year ago… Her husband also recently died. Pilar, she told me I was her daughter. I would always be her daughter. It made Marcos not being there a little easier. I could see where he came from, the *good* that made him. Ysleta, his neighborhood. It's one of the poorest in El Paso, but the Martinez family, they were different. They worked so hard. They loved each other. They worked together. It's the best thing in my life right now. It's what keeps me going. Their little world. They keep me going. Pancho, Marcos's brother, such a good father to my kids, such a good husband. Isela his wife, the best aunt those kids could have. Noah and Sarah, they look like me. Blond, blue eyes, heh, the whole rotten shebang. But they treat them like blood. They *are* Martinez blood. But Pancho…even within the same family, so different from his brother. Not like Marcos at all."

"Oh." Melissa waits a minute, before continuing, glancing at Lori who smiles at her. It's a smile that doesn't want anything, that's not trying to convince anyone of anything, that's not creating a separation between them. "Did you, when you were married, did you ever have issues with your own family? With marrying your husband?"

"Well, no. My mother knew the Martinezes, she liked Marcos, but she died soon after we were married. Breast cancer. And El Paso's different. It's been mostly Hispanic for generations. It's the way it's always been. I am sure there are racists in El Paso, those who don't want their daughters marrying a Mexican, but I would guess they wouldn't stay very long there. Or they wouldn't say much, because, well, your life would be miserable. You're surrounded. That's mostly everybody there, from the richest to the poorest, and everybody else in between."

"*My* mother was the main problem. Decades ago. But she wasn't a racist, really. She wanted me to marry an 'American,' her idea of what an 'American' was, but even then I didn't listen. My husband is Japanese-American. Still Asian, but not Chinese. She was more or less happy with Donald, because my mother saw 'Japanese' as a move up for me. 'Mexican' was a move down, in her eyes. But she didn't know this friend. She never got to meet him." A shiver— fear or excitement?—races up Melissa's spine, releasing an invisible current of energy into the dead airplane air.

"You think you made the right choice? Maybe, well, I shouldn't... sorry. I shouldn't—"

"No, no, really, it's okay. I haven't thought about it, to tell you the truth. For decades...until now. I love my husband Donald. He's been a good father."

"Oh." Lori stares at the wall of the seat in front of her. "That's good."

Captain Blewit from the flight deck. I've asked our crew members to keep their seats for a few extra minutes. We're in for a bumpy ride to El Paso. That's what's reported to us up ahead. A bit of difficult weather. Soon as we find a longer stretch of relatively smooth air, we will begin our beverage service. Please remain seated with your seat belts fastened for your safety, as well as for the safety of those around you. Safety is our watchword at United Airlines. Thank you. I'll have an update for you closer to our destination.

"God, I was hoping it wouldn't be one of those flights." With every bump and tilt, Melissa can feel an acidic ball rising and settling in her throat. She shuts her eyes.

"You okay?"

"I'm fine. Just sometimes… Flown dozens of times. My kids, when they were younger, they used to make fun of me. Gina loves roller coasters. Still does." Melissa grips the arm of her aisle seat with one hand, her fingers splayed, knuckles pink and bony, the plane wobbling in the air from left to right, anything but steady. Melissa imagines their incredible speed forward, hundreds of miles per hour, and at the same time waves of air—currents so powerful they are like invisible, cross-cutting rivers in the sky—threatening to fling the plane from its path. How do these machines keep from being ripped apart? She needs to think about something else.

"It's hard to go against your family."

"Well, yes. So… What was Marcos like? He was in the military? I hope it's okay to—"

"Yes, of course," Lori says, glancing at Melissa again. A sudden thump near her feet startles Melissa. Behind her, she hears what sounds like a sharp bell. Call button? "I was proud of him. Marcos was a leader, that was his best quality. He led an Army supply team. His convoy ran over an IED in the middle of the night. In a sandstorm.

Killed one of his men too. Months later a friend of his sent me a letter about what happened, even called me on the phone, too. Lieutenant Mike Levin. He roomed with Marcos in Fallujah. He was like Marcos, very direct, and hearing him on the phone reminded me of how Marcos talked. Not too many wasted words. But everything true. Honorable. Straight. Like you could believe every word. I guess it's 'military speak,' I heard someone call it once. It's the way they are. It's also the way Marcos was." Lori casually brushes the blond hair from her eyes, as the plane tilts left from side to side, and shudders.

"He sounds like a good man. Very hard to find."

"He was…yes… So your husband's Japanese. And you're…?"

"Chinese. Chinese-American. Born in San Francisco. My parents grew up in Liaoning Province." A scream from the front of the plane, as light flickers through the clouds, like a faulty strobe light. It is a child's scream, a baby crying. That ball of acid in Melissa's throat is about to explode.

"Yee-ao-ing…?"

"Liaoning. North of Beijing. I've never been. But I heard about it all the time from my mother." A man with short-cropped white hair staggers through the tilting aisle—the seat belt sign still on—and turns behind him as an overhead bin snaps open, narrowly missing his head, his thigh inches from Melissa's face. *Jesus.*

"Oh."

"Donald's a lawyer. He's done well. We bought a few rental properties, including his office. The kids are doing well in school, although they don't have an interest in law." The almost mechanical bursts from the screaming and gasping child, somewhere in the front, hit Melissa's chest like invisible pulses of air. She shut her eyes just in time to hear the massive thump of the bathroom door as it seals shut.

"Are you a lawyer too?"

"No, I, I worked for the city of San Francisco before my first, Gina, was born. Then I stayed home to take care of her, and then Bruce. Now I manage these properties. 'Manage' the kids too, if you know what I mean, although it's mostly Bruce now. He'll be in college next year." Melissa exhales deeply, and Lori is gamely smiling at her, but her skin is waxen. Melissa thinks, *When will this awful turbulence stop? Please god.* She finds Lori's skin soothing, inert but soothing: her pallid color seems to radiate "stop," as if a color could utter a sound through its form.

"You're coming from Boston, right?"

"Some friends from graduate school had a reunion of sorts. A long weekend at a yoga retreat. It was a little weird, but I got to see them."

"You went all the way from San Francisco? That's a long way." Lori stares at Melissa for a few more moments, the plane still rocking, but less, buffeted by the heavy clouds. "Was he there? This Hispanic friend you knew a long time ago?"

"Oh, no. Noooo. He wasn't there. No, I didn't go because I thought he would be there. He wasn't." Melissa whiffs an antiseptic stink behind her, and waits for, but hears no sound from the bathroom door behind her and sees no white-haired man stumbling through the aisle. *Just keep looking at this Lori. Why does she seem so calm inside?*

"Oh. That's too bad. Maybe it would've been nice to see how he turned out. What happened to him."

"Well, maybe, yeah. I think so. I don't know why I'm thinking of him now. It's strange. Maybe I did go to Boston, in a way, looking for him. But I have no idea if he even lives there anymore. Is that crazy?"

"No, I don't think so. It's kind of a lingering doubt. I know the feeling."

"That's a good way to put it. Lingering doubt. I knew he wouldn't be there, but in my mind I thought I would revisit our neighborhood, not really intending to see him. Just…to think. You know, men stay put in their minds. A man does that. They would go back to an old neighborhood and expect the woman, the girlfriend, to be there, waiting for him, in the same emotional place he left her years ago. It's kind of a male chauvinism, I think." Melissa tries to feel better: the plane's still rocking, strange scents assault her face, these flickering lights, but she's okay. She can't *wait* to be okay. She will be okay.

"But you weren't doing that."

"No. I knew he wouldn't be there. But I thought, while visiting my friends at the spa retreat, friends who I haven't seen for years — you know we had to eat our breakfast in *silence*? — I thought I could remember why this man mattered to me, why in some way he still does. This 'lingering doubt.' Thank you for that. That's the best way I've been able to put it so far." Melissa exhales deeply, as if she's finished a long run, trying to expel whatever is in her chest, this horrible ride. Lori only smiles at her.

"Well, maybe you're thinking how your life might have been different if you had stayed with him. Is that it?"

"Maybe. It's kind of imagining what it would be. It's also kind of a fantasy too."

"A Mexican-American fantasy."

"Yeah. When I compare the fantasy with my reality, with Donald, Bruce, and Gina, the fantasy often wins." *I'll be fine. I know I'll be fine.*

"Of course. But you didn't live with that man for twenty, twenty-five years. You didn't have kids, you didn't live a life. That dirty, hard life we all go through. I loved Marcos. I still love him. I remember every time we were together. He was, he was…beyond passionate. But it was also hard. Sometimes we fought. I didn't want him to re-enlist and I never told him that. I felt I had no right. He had a kind of sense of purpose in the military. Knew who he was. That's my only regret. That I didn't tell him. He died and he shouldn't have died. I believe we would have worked everything out between us. At home. That's my fantasy, I guess."

Lori appears beyond calm to Melissa, which is startling to her. She takes a moment to process what Lori has said and feels a mixture of awe and jealousy for this stranger's composure. Inside Melissa's head, she's on a boat, this boat plummeting and rising in a heavy sea, no land in sight, and the boat is *in the air*, thousands and thousands of feet above nothing.

"We do whatever we need to keep going. I think that's it. At the end of the road, at the end of the road…" Melissa exhales again, and imagines a sickening green mist floating from her mouth.

"…is El Paso, hah. You'll be able to see the star on the mountain when we get closer. If it's not too cloudy." Lori's face is turned to the window. What brings Melissa out of herself again: she can see Lori's crying in silence.

"You know, it's not your fault…"

"I know. I know that. At first I did blame myself for not saying anything. But then I stopped. You can't live backwards. You can't live perfectly, knowing what will happen before it does, and making every decision like that. But your mind kind of tortures you anyway. Lieutenant Levin sent another letter…something I wished I'd never read…but no…That doesn't matter anyway… Marcos should've been home. He wanted to be with me."

Around them the world steadies itself again. And this time it stays that way.

The flight attendants have walked through the aisle already, the baby has stopped screaming, and Melissa can see the food cart wending its way from the front toward them. The line of sight down the aisle of Flight 4165, this empty space—an invisible portent of disaster when it rocked and tilted—is transformed now into an anchor for their safe passage, as steady and straight as could be. Melissa inhales deeply and releases a last lingering air of unease inside her. She thinks about her bed of tulips, scheduling the new water heater installation, driving home to San Francisco with her daughter. Arriving home at the end of this day to end all days.

In the same moment as before, Lori continues, the tears now wiped away from her cheeks, facing Melissa. "So why do you think you still think of him?"

This is the captain from the flight deck. Looks like we'll have a nice ride to El Paso from here. It might get a little bumpy when we begin our initial descent. But it should be mostly fine, and I'll let you know before, so everybody gets a chance to stretch their legs one last time before we land. But it should be a smooth ride from here. Please keep your seat belts buckled, in case we encounter any unexpected turbulence. Give your attention and courtesy to

the finest flight attendants in the skies. We appreciate your business at United
Airlines. Thank you.

Melissa thinks of all the time she now has, before the next leg of her trip. "If you don't mind… I'm just… I'm taking a nap for an hour. I may have a long night ahead of me in El Paso or Los Angeles." She smiles cursorily at her companion.

"Oh, yes. Of course."

Melissa closes her eyes and imagines being in California, on the ground, and imagines gardening and the sunshine, and any lingering questions seem to dissipate in the steady air and the nice chatter around her and Lori's quiet presence next to her. Melissa will be home after El Paso. It will be nice to visit the desert southwest for a few hours. In the darkness behind her eyelids, she thinks she hears her neighbor sniffling in the background, wills herself not to open her eyes. She can't wait to get home.

LIBRARY ISLAND

"Shipment #16 on its way, Arturo—"

I panic as soon as I detect the blue electronic monitor near my door. Stacks of books in boxes litter my cell like a disorganized warehouse. My back throbs with pain. In the next cell, I overhear Jacqueline, I know it is Jacqueline, pleading with her interlocutor.

"I can't do this! It's too much! It's inhumane! How do you expect us—"

A thud…and silence, as I imagine she has been struck in the head, her mouth taped. Perhaps she has been drugged again. I hear the low screech of more duct tape as they maybe wrap it around her legs. I hear a few knocks on the door or the wall as she struggles or maybe as they clumsily carry her to the hallway. I want to scream, "Leave her alone!" but I say nothing. Will they put someone else in her place, another refugee wanting in to this sanctuary?

I jam the newly issued purple earplugs in my ears. I don't want to imagine—as I try to read my next book as quickly and carefully as I can, with six finished in two days—what the guards might do to Jacqueline, what an officer in charge of entry and exit might do, once she is helpless and alone. Yes, these are extraordinary times. In my throat, a tide of vomit surges and recedes. Outside I met Jacqueline, but briefly, and in our cells I waited for her voice at night, as we talked before falling asleep from our reading exhaustion. Jacqueline possessed a high-pitched, delicate voice, and its disembodied song and cadence took me far away from this place. Now I am torn with heartache about her, and my mind is my worst enemy, yet I have to survive. I imagine her auburn hair and athletic body, the blue sweater she wore that day in the forest, a librarian's sweater. I imagine we are surrounded by books, but not here, never here. I imagine a future reading together for our monthly re-tests as "island citizens," and that leisurely exchange of ideas with her, and holding her hands as friends. Our warmth released to each other, once we are ready and safe for our re-tests. Our fingers tracing the most delicate contours of our veins. A respite, just before we start another month of reading. A life slipped in between the only work that matters. All this, just dreams from my memories of her voice. Even now she saves me. *Jacqueline*. The images I have of her in mind, my secret hope. I do not hear them dragging her body out. I do not hear the cell door slam shut next to mine. Dear God, I never really knew Jacqueline well. Now I never will. In this stale air, I feel like I am choking.

Seven of us are on this floor. I think it's seven cells next to each other. I believe I have heard seven distinct voices through the barred portal of my door. How many more in this building? How many have stumbled upon these gates, or approached these walls, or have been captured on the beach, all in search of Library Island? Is that even the name of this place? They tell you nothing when you are captured. They tell you nothing as you begin your tests for citizenship. They tell you only what you must do, the impossible entry requirements, the severe penalties, the telos of existence you must achieve, and maintain, forever.

I may be next for my fifteenth test, fifteen boxes, each with twenty-five books, a dreaded knock and red flash at my door—it has been about ten days. Fourteen distinct interlocutors (another on the way) have quizzed me about each box of twenty-five books. I do not know who they are. I know we are being watched. Fourteen times they have smiled wanly at me, in my disheveled state, my eyes glassy and rimmed darkly by lack of sleep, my back beset with mini-spasms from sitting on my ass for hours. I do not lack for food, I do not lack for warmth, I am like a terrorized, well-fed rat inside this cell. What I need is rest and sleep—and more time without threats. What I need is peace of mind. What I need is to think of Jacqueline. Poor Jacqueline. What am I becoming?

I have begun to read standing up and then sitting down. You would think this would drain you even more, but on the contrary. I read better, and I am ready when they knock at the door. I am getting stronger, strangely, in this overcast sky of fatigue. My notes printed clearly. My body in service to my mind. My body cleansed of the nervous anarchy of the Outer World. My mind more efficient than it has ever been. Is that it? Perhaps that is exactly what the interlocutors want, who they will allow in. How many more tests? I don't know. Dear god, help me. I will be ready for the next one. I have even had time to re-read books I am not sure about. I will not faint from exhaustion. My body is hungry to escape this cell, but my mind is sharper than ever. In our night conversations, I never told Jacqueline of my standing-up trick, and others, to help me endure our torture.

What have I become? Maybe I could have saved her. I should have tried to save her. But why should I not fight for myself? What if we are being pitted against each other in a foul competition? We do not know anything. What if they choose only a certain number? They told us nothing when they captured us. What if only one of us was meant to survive? What have I done?

"They said the exact opposite last week!" my friend Edward had screamed at the telemonitor months before. "Do they think we're that moronic?" The anchors of The News of the World were reporting that the economy was in tatters because "illegal invaders from outside the company territory" were trying to destabilize the city in a convoluted plot to replace and even kill "native born residents." This news channel was now number one in the city, especially after the company revoked the licenses of its two main competitors. "Arturo, Chris, are you listening to this?"

"Turn it off, please," Chris pleaded. The telemonitor showed roving gangs breaking windows of "storefronts owned by illegals, undesirables, corrupt foreigners." The News anchors smiled as they reported the mayhem on the streets. The helicopter camera came up close to a group of five men surrounding a taxi, punching the driver who seemed to be wearing a turban. They dragged him out of the vehicle as the car slowly rolled forward, the dark-skinned man pleading with his arms in the air, gesticulating to the backseat. Blood poured from his forehead. One man kicked the driver's face as he fell. Still rolling across the intersection, the taxi first hit the knee and then ran over the torso of one the attackers, as if consuming him like a languid, yellow monster. Others chased the couple stumbling from the taxi's backseat into an abandoned building, off camera. The voice from The News: "Another devastating, native-born death caused by people who do not belong in this territory."

"Edward, turn it off. Please, do we have to see this? It's like a violent porno," Chris said.

"Someone threw a brick at my head in the subway today," I said. "I was on my phone, checking the WalkSafe app about where it was okay to go. I heard a scream behind me. Thank god for that woman. I looked up just as I saw his arm release the brick. I ducked just in time." I trembled involuntarily, my mind taking me back to the moment. Over the past few months, the chaos around the city had intensified in waves. This past week had been another series of nightmares, more stores closing, mysterious armed guards at the front of grocery stores, certain co-ops, including ours, and even museums.

"Where the hell are the company militias?" Chris said, holding his boyfriend's hand, but Edward pushed him away as he concentrated on The News. I remember that I wanted to hold *both* their hands at the moment: they were the only friends I could count on in the city, and I had often invited them for Friday night cocktails and a movie in my apartment. We had been born at the edge of the edge of a crumbling world.

"Sense has become nonsense, and these phones, these technologies, are at the root of it all. Was anyone looking at each other on the subway? Anyone talking to their neighbor anymore? It's the little, fake, distorted worlds we've created with these malevolent, addictive machines," Edward said, glancing at the telemonitor and then turning his piercing hazel eyes at Chris and me. I blushed.

Edward continued: "Not you, Arturo. Of course, not you. But just look at us. We're obsessed with clicking 'Hates' and 'Loves,' and that's what we've become!" I noticed his foot was pumping hard against the wooden floors of my apartment. I had heard a version of this diatribe before. "Those have become our reasons, arguments, beliefs! That's all we do! Why is it surprising that we've reduced each other to these stupidities? Why is it surprising that we are so easily manipulated by The News, the company, or whoever peddles another spectacular outrage? We've all become simpletons, reactive vessels, vengeful trolls—"

"Loin-pumping idiots. That's my favorite," Chris said, which almost prompted a smile from Edward, but also deflated him somewhat. At least for a few seconds. I also smiled at Chris because he knew his Edward, the philosophy major, the activist, fearless to the point of sometimes being foolhardy.

"Damn right! What happened to our brains? These goddamn machines have destroyed our reasoning. We have to get out of here before it's too late." He clicked off the telemonitor. "Arturo, read this."

He handed me what looked like a manuscript, perhaps thirty pages, with typewritten text aligned around crude, out-of-focus photos in black and white. In large type at the top, it read *"Common Sense."*

"It's an underground newsletter from the neighborhood," Chris said quickly. "Keep it. We have a few copies Edward picked up in front of what's left of the public library on Amsterdam."

"The real news. But look here," Edward said, first tugging and then grabbing the stapled pages back and flipping to a page toward the back of what felt like a parchment to me, a relic of the days of newspapers and physical books, before electronic media, before social media, before the short tweets of 'news' that were now the written word, if it was written at all. Most of the 'news' was manufactured images and mindless talk now. "Read this, Arturo. It's about Library Island. It may not exist, and the way they describe it, this place may not even be an island but somewhere in the rural west, a hidden fortress city, a sanctuary, but if it does exist Chris and I are going there. You should come with us. This will be your last chance to escape this madness."

"You're leaving? When?" I asked. I remembered that when I heard what Edward said, the words on the page suddenly became blurry, and I couldn't think. I did not want to be alone, and I did not want to be without my friends. I sat down on my sofa to breathe, to not stumble onto the coffee table, to absorb what was happening.

"Soon. As soon as we can," Chris said. "In the next few days, after we've put everything in storage, what's valuable, after we talk to a few more friends."

"For how long?"

"Forever."

These days, my last days in The Outer World. I had searched for the words "Library Island" after my conversation with Edward and Chris. I saw my super, who had been talking to the guards at the front of our co-op. Strangely they were in the middle of positioning a barricade in front of our door to the street. Three massive concrete blocks, Jersey highway dividers, had been stacked in front of the door at an angle. About one block away, a car smoldered after being torched last night.

"Hey, Arturo. You hear what happened to Edward? In 1810. Aren't you friends with him?" Rafael Dooley said. "He was shot two blocks away."

"Edward? Shot? Oh my god!" My knees buckled. The armed guards looked at me oddly, as if they were seeing a ghost. "They shot him? Who shot him? Is he okay?"

Rafael looked at me, not quite teary, his mouth about to say some words, but they just wouldn't come out. I knew the answer to my question. I felt a palpitation in my chest. If I had been alone, if I didn't have these men around me, I would have collapsed on our sidewalk. No one else was on the street. "I'm sorry, Arturo. No. He died. Chris, his friend, he hasn't come back either. I know he was at the hospital with Edward. This morning he called us at the front desk, sobbing. I don't know where Chris is. If you see him, if you see him, ask him… I don't know if we can do anything."

"What happened? My god." I felt dizzy, but I needed to know. I needed to know.

"This is what I heard. From what Chris told us. But also Alicia, in 710, she said she was there, in the crowd that was coming out of the subway. She was coming back home too. A group of men surrounded Edward and Chris. Edward started arguing with them. Alicia said it was something about his wire-rimmed glasses, but she also said they, Edward and Chris, were holding hands. Something, someone started an argument right outside the subway. With a gang. You can't be out at night. You know that, right? Unless it's an emergency. You can't. Not anymore. It's too dangerous. Anyway, they were arguing, Edward pushed someone to get them away from Chris. And they shot Edward. They shot him."

"I, I, I can't believe it. Edward? Why did he argue with them?" I wanted to see if I could find Chris. I wanted to leave. I wanted to scream. The sun was bright on the street, the smoke from the fires did not choke me too much, and the quiet on 86th Street seemed oddly peaceful, portentous. The guards turned away from me. Only Rafael kept staring at me.

"It's dangerous out there. You can't be alone. You can't be out at night anymore. I've told all the residents. They know. Let me know if you locate Chris, if we can help him somehow. Arturo…Arturo. You okay?"

"I just…I just can't believe it. I need to find Chris. Thank you, Rafael. Thank you for telling me."

"We have a resident meeting tomorrow. Eight p.m. Don't forget. We're setting up the volunteer schedule."

I couldn't breathe. The lump in my throat seemed to grow as I walked into my apartment and locked the door. Not a few days ago, Edward and Chris had been right there, on the couch. I started crying, I looked out the window, I wanted to jump through the glass, I wanted to fly away from all of this madness, I wanted to escape. How could they have killed Edward? Who? Just a gang? What were we becoming? What was happening to our city, our country? I kept trying to remember Edward's face, his passion for causes, how being good mattered to him, and how he made it matter to us. Mobs torching neighborhoods. The mysterious firebombing of street leaders. Random attacks against the weak. The hunt for those who were different. The disappearance of moral boundaries. A war of all against all. Edward had been right. For months, Edward had warned us. I looked up at the blue sky over the Hudson River. I tried to imagine Edward as the archangel Gabriel flying to heaven.

I never found Chris. That night, the day after Edward died, a mob killed Chris in front of the Lucerne Hotel on Amsterdam Avenue. They beat him to death. The same gang? I never knew. Maybe Chris went looking for who had done this to his beloved, maybe nothing mattered to him anymore. The clerk at the front desk informed me, after I asked if he had heard anything more about Edward and Chris. I felt like he had punched me in the gut, this clerk. The building was emptying out, he also said, many people were leaving, escaping the city. His eyes did not seek me out as Rafael's did. This clerk did not know Edward or Chris, this clerk a new employee after Vincent, the regular daytime clerk, had left. This clerk was a stranger among us. What he said to me, he said as if he were reporting a trash spill on the roadway. I was more alone than ever on the eastern edge of what was once called the United States of America.

I visited several impromptu markets during the day, with rare delicacies like strawberries and chocolate, staples like rice and bread rolls, but could not find a more recent copy of Edward and Chris's *Common Sense*. I went to the old public library and nothing was there but a heap of burnt books. On the telemonitor I heard "news" about the border city where I was born (thousands of miles from 86th Street), where much of my family still lived in fear. Comely newscasters smirked as they said, "These invading hordes bring diseases. They want what we have. They're vermin begetting more vermin." Long ago, I had once believed when watching The News of the World that these newscasters badly disguised a political agenda. I had been sure of it. But it had taken me years to understand, it had taken Edward's words for me to appreciate that these well-groomed pretties lusted only for conflict, for any attack against another, as long as that "Other" was a target, as long as The News could revel in these images. I couldn't stop the tears and the anger when I watched The News. Edward's and Chris's deaths merited not even a mention. I turned off the telemonitor. I remembered the way Edward laughed with a soft snort at the end. Chris taking Edward's hand mid-swing on our walks together. How they lost themselves in each other's eyes...

I kept telling myself I should have listened to Edward's words: "I'll never set up a social media account. It's garbage! Who cares. I'd rather talk to you. Do you really think it means anything to have one hundred pings?" But even I could not abandon social media completely. I casually pressed a "Love" button to the page of an honorable politician who criticized the shooting of dark-skinned laborers as they sprinted across international borders. The News of the World kept a body count they published every Thursday, a tally of undesirables eliminated at border entry points. Smaller news channels denounced these killings. I worried about my mother as I kept searching for news on Library Island.

That week I decided to visit my ailing mother in my hometown of El Paso. On an adobe wall, I saw spray-painted "Cosio Torgerson, dead!" He was the politician who had spoken up earlier. I wondered if this was protest graffiti or if I had missed the news. *Chris would have sent me a notice already. Edward would have been ready to spend all night talking about it*, I thought, my heart still in pieces. These were extraordinary times, and I was alone. I was walking not far from the river of the old southwestern border of our country, on my way to buy a bag of chile to bring back. My childhood neighborhood now nominally in the nation of Texas. Without warning, a Doberman pinscher lunged at me from behind dead bushes and sunk its teeth into my calf. I screamed. Steps behind the dog, an old friend yanked the animal back by a collar. I cursed and shouted at him to drive me to a hospital, yet Roberto only grinned at me and sputtered that that's what I deserved "for loving Cosio Torgerson." Roberto Murillo—my heart still pounding like a hammer in my chest, rivulets of blood from my calf soaking through my jeans—I remembered vaguely as a friend from grade school, whom I had added recently to my social network. I was stunned. I hadn't spoken to him in years! I had become a tourist on my childhood street. He had never left this godforsaken dust. I had been so stupid, so naïve. I was a stranger in my neighborhood, just as to many I would always be a stranger in the social ether. Would I dare contact the weak and corrupt local militia for help? I limped to my mother's house, and as I cleaned my superficial wound, I understood how our old world was not even a mere whisper anymore. I certainly did not want to live where I had been born. I also did not want to stay in the big city on the coast where I had escaped years ago. Christopher's and Edward's city. Nowhere was safe. I did not tell my mother what had happened two blocks from her home. I drove myself to an emergency room within her company's district. I imagined an old adobe wall falling on Roberto Murillo and his dog and crushing both of them to death.

Back at 86th Street, I remembered Edward's last words to me, and I cataloged all references to Library Island. The mentions and rumors. The supposed photographs from outside its walls. The guesses to its secret location. The gossip was that the brightest minds had established this new world. They had taken the most advanced technology and weaponry to protect it against the hordes of the Outer World. "Library soldiers" had sabotaged, and were sabotaging, the existential weaponry abandoned in the Outer World. They had left behind only the small arms, as powerful and as ubiquitous as they were. Buffer zones of hundreds of miles—newsletters claimed—detected any outsiders attempting to reach Library Island. The peaceful and intelligent were presumably allowed in, no matter their politics. Other rumors suggested that the children of Library Island had to pass grueling reading tests—and all adults too. Any failure would mean expulsion. Some newsletters hinted at disappearances and executions, all in the name of preserving this sanctuary. Strange and arbitrary "Basic Principles" were rigorously obeyed within Library Island. Were these rumors and half-truths the work of propagandists of the Outer World, or Library Island?

I packed my most precious belongings, which weren't many. Sentimental items, mostly photos of my mother and dead father and one favorite photo of Edward, Chris, and me at the old Anchor Bar in New Haven. I closed any accounts that still mattered and forwarded all my correspondence to my mother and sent her a letter telling her what I would do. By special courier, I also sent my mother three items of value she might be able to trade to help her in a crisis. Whether she ever received them would not matter, yet I believed the chances were good that she did. I flew on one of the safe flights to a remote town in the west, where *Common Sense* had hinted about inexplicable discoveries, sensors in trees, dozens of disappearances, bodies—what looked like bodies—in shallow graves.

I traveled by night, paying those who would be willing to take me further west. I was stranded in several one-stop hamlets and spent weeks hiking through mountain ranges and around gorges. I met others whom I befriended and trusted only after spending time with them, all of us on this same elusive mission to find Library Island. I kept seeing Chris's and Edward's faces in the trees. I believed they were with me. They will always be with me. After weeks together, our small group beheld flashes in the night. What looked like campfires across a few hills. One night a new friend Jacqueline joined us, also searching for what we had been searching for. We shared our food and supplies with her. One day after that night in a western forest, both of us had been captured by what appeared to be night patrols from Library Island. *We are close to its edges. Almost there. The rumors are true, and have always been true*, I thought. These guards did not hurt us, but they bound our hands and pulled black hoods over our faces and uttered assurances that we would be given a chance to prove ourselves. I was frightened, yet in a way also elated. After what seemed three or four days of travel, after a deep sleep that later I believed had been induced with drugs in our food, we awoke in our cells. Next to each other. They assumed Jacqueline and I had been a couple, their only mistake. We were and we were not together.

What was life like inside? I could only imagine. We had seen nothing but the walls of our cells. What little I understood was that the overseers of Library Island—our captors said so few words to us—were trying to tear us away from the Outer World. Every bit of you, the seen and the unseen "you." This cleansing, through books. If I could survive that, if I could endure… What I saw in the eyes of my interlocutors was reason mixed with madness. Reason: it was clear what new entrants had to do—if I could explain and better argue for or against a book, to demonstrate that I had read it, then they would move on to the next book. If I could not, if I missed *one* book, if an interlocutor indicated I had failed to "read" a book, as subjective as I first imagined that evaluation could be, I would be immediately expelled. The madness? No second chances. No appeals to a higher authority. Months ago, those were the only instructions I had received an hour before my first shipment arrived at my cell door. The same instructions repeated before every new shipment arrived. The guards outside my cell were monoliths, with eyes never acknowledging my presence, silences like rocky shoals for any pleas for explanations. I imagined the power with which my friend Edward would have attacked these tasks, I believed in Edward and the idea of his mind, I transformed myself into who I think Edward would be proud of...

All my interlocutors were sophisticated readers, and it was not a uniformity of opinion they were seeking. No book had a jacket cover. Interlocutors had read the books in my shipment too. They asked for a nuanced view of each book, a viewpoint based on details about characters or scenes or writing style, or better, questions and possibilities posed by the book to the reader, and in reality, all of the above. At the beginning, these interlocutors, men and women, seemed astoundingly severe and circumspect and said nothing other than to ask questions about my books. I guessed that the first ten interlocutors expected me to fail, were waiting for me to fail, as perhaps many did. I tried to gain any information about Library Island, the process, how long it would take, why we had been locked up like criminals. Always, after two minutes, I had been warned that unless I returned to answering questions about my books, and only my books, if I persisted on these irrelevant inquiries, my answer for the record would constitute a "Non-answer." Also known as "Failure." I knew from looking into their eyes that after more than two minutes of protests, they would stand up, they would walk out my cell door, and they would cross a point of no return. I did not ever dare to protest past the two-minute mark. Lately I had stopped asking anything and just gave them the answers they wanted. I was confronting a System. This System had no mercy, no bend, no leeway, nothing but obedience to its "Basic Principles." I could break against this System, and they would not blink an eye. Like Jacqueline.

Words seemed to matter again. I lost myself in the different worlds of books for hours at a time. Slowly I became better at my work, beyond anything I imagined Edward would have accomplished. I wrote notes, not to forget my impressions as I read night after night. They had provided writing materials with the first shipment. In the cell next to mine, Jacqueline always received a different set of twenty-five books. I developed a certain consistency of the mind. A disposition to talk and consider and weigh empathetically. We were fed nutritious if bland meals, we exercised in our rooms, and we received shipment after shipment, with ten-day deadlines for our tests with interlocutors.

After about the fourth or fifth shipment, I was exhausted. My head felt constantly hot, as if consumed by a low-grade fever. I dreamt about books and their stories. I woke up and immediately started reading every morning. I did nothing else for hours and hours. At a certain point, my eyeballs felt as if they were popping out of their sockets. Then I recovered. I had no choice but to gather myself.

Through this pain, strangely, I became stronger. I created tricks to help me endure. I kept reading and writing notes desperately, as Jacqueline sobbed in her cell next to me many nights. I pushed through my fatigue with fear. Did she not have a hero to guide her like my Edward? I obsessed about how I could change what I did, the little I did in my cell, to become a better reader, to transform myself into a great reader, to destroy any book-obstacle in front of me. I decided I would rather die reading, and remembering what I read, than be defeated by any box, by any question posed by my merciless, stone-faced interlocutors. I would rather my mind explode. I believe the root of this strength of will came from my mother and father, from the work they taught me to do in the borderlands, the work that had broken many backs, the work that was a scream against the desert dust, this work that taught me about the song of nothingness in my bones and why the only way to live was to die on my feet. As the early sun in my imprisoned universe, Edward focused my reading through bouts of exhaustion, and transformed this will into, into…

I hear a perfunctory knock at my door. The lock turns and the long bolt shrieks open. My new interlocutor steps into my cell. I am ready.

Test for Shipment #15. After my eighth book, I stop mid-explanation and plead with my interlocutor: "What would really happen if I didn't read a book, if you say I can't adequately explain it? Did you go through this? When does this stop?" I have asked these questions many times, but it is the first time I receive more than just a strained smile, silence or a warning. Her eyes seem even kind. My heart flutters in my chest, a sparrow trapped underneath armor.

"Let's go to the next one."

"I don't even know your name. I get a new person every shipment. Please, just a few answers."

The woman looks behind her, waits, "seeing" with her ears through the door's portal. I appreciate her appearance for the first time, through the swells of my fear and anger. She is athletic, in a fitted navy blue dress. Auburn hair, like Jacqueline's, but a touch darker. Green eyes behind black librarian's glasses. Freckles dot her cheeks and cover her neck. My bone-deep exhaustion envelops my head like an invisible mask, and I almost fall forward in my chair. Have they placed her here because of what happened to Jacqueline? We hear the guard's footsteps in the hallway, but he is not visible. "It's Elizabeth," she whispers. "Just keep going. You have made remarkable progress and are already showing signs of permanent mental change. Can't say anything else. You are almost there."

"Permanent change? What—"

"Let's keep going."

"Thank you for telling me your name. It's been so long…please… Elizabeth. What if I collapse and die of a heart attack? I can't keep going forever. I will until I can't, I will until…" I do find her beautiful, yet so far away from where I am. I feel disgusting next to her, disheveled. I am a rock trying not to be crushed to bits, she is a jewel shining through time. I stare just a second too long at her shapely body and at those cat eyes against the pallid skin. She blushes. I convince myself her eyes glisten with a certain longing without words. I convince myself she believes in me, this awful me, this wretch, she just might believe…

"Don't. I mean, 'Don't collapse.' The next one." Elizabeth turns her head again to the portal and whispers, "It's easier once you are a citizen. You still have reading. You must do the mental work every month. But you gain an appeals process. A second chance, if something goes wrong. You gain your freedom among us. You can live with someone, who must also read, and that helps. It's much easier. You'll see. Arturo—"

"Elizabeth, what happens?"

"They get rid of you."

"You mean they release you? To the Outer World?"

"They get rid of you. Expunged. You will never have existed."

"They kill you? Is that what happened to Jacqueline? I mean, how can they—you—justify that? How…isn't this an island of reason, of sanity? What is the difference between this and the Outer World, my god!"

"Arturo, keep your voice down. We will both be in trouble. Everything is monitored, but I think there's a certain leeway granted to those beyond fifteen shipments. You are there. She almost made it. That's beyond your control. You have to understand and appreciate what we have achieved. What we will protect. At all costs." Behind Elizabeth's beauty radiates a quiet ferocity and stillness, an uncanny self-possession…the timbre in her voice still echoes in my ears. She stares at a corner of the room where a triangle of black glass shimmers in the half-light. For the first time, I notice a palpitating green dot at the center of this triangle.

"They kill you?"

"Worse than that…much worse. I like you, Arturo. Please don't give up. If you make it, I will look for you. I also work at the integration center," she says. The sudden terror in her eyes jolts my heart to a faster beat. "Let's keep going." A neon red dot glows inside the triangle. I think of only Elizabeth, the details of her movements, the sounds of her voice, as I answer her questions. I am answers, only for her.

Reading is doing. Reading is doing, I repeat in my head months later. Three a.m. and I was asleep, but not anymore. My dear Elizabeth is next to me. The darkness outside absolute. On Library Island every home is separated by a few acres. Our numbers permit us this luxury. The separation also prevents noise from interfering with our reading work, prevents also too much interaction with others beyond our household, except for our weekly community meetings and discussions and assignments of service, these akin to "jobs" in the Outer World, but here are services only to benefit our community. "Library Island" is just a nickname, but officially we are the "City of the Immortals." In about two years, I must enlist in my first tour of military service, which might include forays into the Outer World to manage and undermine it. We do not lack for food, and our home is repaired when necessary. We have no "money," the strangest adjustment from my previous life, but one that now makes perfect sense. We exist not to grow, not to profit, not to advance technologically (although a certain advantage must always be maintained over our enemies), but to resist the Outer World, to survive as it slowly destroys itself. To be vigilant for permutations of other Outer Worlds beyond our borders. We will fight to protect what we have achieved.

The reading work is less than the citizenship test, with more time to ponder our work. My first monthly shipments have focused on many, but not all, books written by our scribes about where we are now, where we could be, where we were. Generations ago it began when one group, and its allies, believed their blood was the source of their greatness, rather than the fortune of history, rather than the success of their brutality on others... Our history began when others challenged these first pioneers and defeated them in simple and more profound ways... It all began when the rules and norms established by these first groups were weakened, abandoned, and finally overturned, when the principle of non-contradiction was annihilated in word and deed. When evil elites exploited a weakened society to keep power. When we stopped being a "we." When "moral virtue" collapsed into "doing whatever you could get away with." When 'thinking' became whatever prejudice and fear we shared. When "the education of citizenry" metamorphosed into a culture overrun by images and reactions to them. At a certain tipping point, the Outer World even forgot humans and thinking could have been any different: they entered a gulag in which its inhabitants did not even recognize their squalid imprisonment. In an eloquent way, these books confirmed my suspicions: being born at the edge of the edge of a disastrous world had kept me from losing myself in it. Edward, my dearest Edward, and Chris, and so many others, they were casualties of this war. I understand our history now. In a way I am returning to my old self as a student of philosophy, one of many outsiders from the borderlands. As I read as I have never read before, I have a sense I am approaching a strange Infinity: my individuality is fulfilled, while oddly, my self is obliterated. Yet I will never forget my friends.

Perhaps I could write a book, too, for our citizenry. I would focus on how reading has opened my eyes, how it has allowed me to consider the many different, even contradictory, views in history. It is this very process of deeply spending time with an idea to consider complexities that has changed me. In town, on my walks, I listen as I have never listened before, even to those I know I probably have little in common with. They listen too: they are also readers. Perhaps what we have in common is that our heads are hot with thinking and possibilities and connections beyond our bodies, beyond the here and now. It's not that our bodies don't matter, or that appearances don't matter, but as a community of readers our bodies and appearances have their importance limited by our minds. Perhaps such a book has already been written, but I know I could give it a unique voice to make it come alive today. A voice from the borderlands. This would help the newest refugees in our city, those whose kin are too often the enslaved and the murdered of the Outer World. For the other Edwards of the world, yes, a voice for them.

Reading is doing, I think in this cold darkness, as I stare at Elizabeth asleep, whom I made love to last night, who has been so earnest and kind these past months, whom I always dream about, besides my books for my monthly re-tests. Elizabeth, so uninhibited, Elizabeth… so confident and cool on the outside, with another self she shares with me inside these walls. I stare at her auburn hair, which spreads over the pillow like a dark red sea anemone on sand, her bare shoulder paler than her face. I remember three moles on her neck, which last night I imagined were secret dark worlds I could explore with my lips. This muscly and ardent Elizabeth has saved every bit of me. I thrive on Elizabeth's tenacity and power. Elizabeth, my new sun.

Her books are on one side of our bedroom and mine on the other, and we do talk about them as we ready ourselves for our re-tests with separate interlocutors each month. We do chores together, we visit friends, but the reading work consumes us. Tonight I imagine floating out of bed without waking Elizabeth. I imagine my body one with the night, free. I notice her black glasses on her nightstand and one of her books splayed on the floor, its pages like white blades, one corner of a pillow delicately bending two pages. *Writing is doing.* I want to wake her, but I don't.

I escape our bed without disturbing my beloved's sleep. Through a window I stare at the cold nothingness of the forest. I do not know exactly where we are, but I know it is west, west of the Outer World, west of the old cities, west in the mountains and beyond. In the hinterland, Jacqueline was lost. In the Outer World, so were Edward, Chris… The earth defeated them, as it will all of us, but some may touch immortality before we die, and touching it is all we can do. We have a monitor for reports, but I have little desire to turn the monitor on. The alert button is not blinking, so there is nothing our community needs to know immediately.

Time has slowed considerably for me, that is what I notice most from my life in the Outer World. My dear Elizabeth has been a citizen for five years, and she says she doesn't remember how time was different outside the City of the Immortals. What is also different is that I am not overwhelmed by any quotidian dread. I can walk our streets in town and lose myself in the smallest leaf or colony of ants. I do not struggle with images of my random slaughter. Tomorrow is an achievement if I am able to lose myself in thought for hours. I expect to die, yes, but not yet. I worry about my re-test, yes, but I know this is the 'essential task,' as they call it, something I can do, what fortifies my citizenship, what makes me worthy to be on Library Island. This is what binds us together as a society. We are the people who read books.

Most of all what is different is my growing disdain for the thoughtless masses of the Outer World. We receive reports of their worst atrocities on each other. They are not 'persons' to me anymore, and I know that sounds harsh. Elizabeth understands, but she does not use such language. Perhaps in time I will not either. Those outside of Library Island are like that Doberman pinscher that attacked me, capable of causing damage for no reason, wild creatures with certain limited powers, human animals trapped within their basest instincts. I also pity them, because I know some have the capability to live beyond the Outer World, just as I did, just as Jacqueline almost did, just as Edward could have done if he only had been given the chance. But too many have not escaped themselves. Instead they have only reveled in their bloody nihilism.

Reading is doing. My back hurts from sitting in my chair and reading for six hours every day. I lie on the carpet and stretch my back in the dark, as I think about whether I should read tonight, with my Elizabeth softly snoring a few feet away. We always eat together, and I notice, too, I choose my words more carefully now, the life inside my mind vibrant, insistent, essential as never before. Elizabeth and I also run together. She calls this "keeping the right balance." I know that after our runs, we both read more vigorously. Our bodies feeding our minds. Our minds nurturing our bodies. I don't think I have been happier in my life.

I know sordid work must be done to protect our sacred haven. We must, to a point, emulate our enemy. We also know the danger of only becoming whom we fight. I know that one day perhaps we will not be successful. One day we may be overrun by the Outer World. Or maybe one day I will fail my re-test as Jacqueline did, and I will fail every appeal, and I will face what I must face. But right now, reading, with Elizabeth next to me, I feel I have reached my place in eternity, my mind one with the matter of the stars above.

If we can only keep the mortal beasts at bay.

CARMELITA TORRES

Arturo, why are you obsessed with this auburn-haired seventeen-year-old who lived two hundred years ago? You have only but a sketch in an old newspaper, *The El Paso Morning Times*, which has turned to dust like all newspapers. At least the overseers of Library Island have preserved this history in the greatest of libraries in North America under their protection. You have but one day when this maid from Juárez raised her voice in protest, January 28, 1917. One day when it mattered for but a few hours to stop traffic between what was then Mexico and the United States, because she did not want to be deloused with gasoline on that international bridge, because she did not want nude photographs of her displayed in border bars by immigration agents of the old United States, as they had with other *mujeres* slaving away for the rich in El Paso, Texas, both brown and white. Why is it that we pile indignities on the most vulnerable? Why do we blame them for our failures, our diseases, our imaginary evils? Is there a bottom to the abyss of our cruelty? Could you turn this history into your first book? Could you teach them, Scholar? Can teaching still be done in this nihilistic world? Or is your voice from the borderlands too late?

Maybe you, Scholar, are in love with your subject, Carmelita Torres. With her auburn hair that reminds you of Jacqueline and

Elizabeth? With that young woman you imagine you could have possessed without enslaving? With that precious defiance which you have always found attractive, that bravery that takes your breath away, that stubbornness a part of you as well, all of it reminding you of these forgotten women and what could have been, if only they had lived in another time, alongside other men? It can't be too late. Even if it is too late, there is no choice but to try to reach the new refugees.

Scholar, if you are being truthful with yourself, you know Carmelita Torres also reminds you of your *bistatarabuelita*, Doña Lola. Your great-great-great grandmother, *la revolucionaria* and *Villista*, a teenage contemporary of Carmelita. Perhaps in your imagination they were friends, Carmelita and Lola. But no, they could not have been friends, because Lola, also a teenager then, lived in rural El Charco near Chihuahua City, not the border town of Juárez. They were both teenagers, yes, during the Mexican Revolution that began in 1910. They were both in the state of Chihuahua, yes, a few hundreds of miles apart, but in different worlds. They were both admirers of Francisco Villa and his *División del Norte*, because who in those hinterlands wasn't if you didn't want to be dead? Carmelita and Lola were both alive at the same moment, yes, and that precious fact will always separate you from them. You are alive now, after all of that history is gone and turned to dust.

The young Lola had shot and killed two men who attempted to rape her—at least according to family lore. You also know from family archives that Doña Lola lived until her mid-eighties in El Segundo Barrio in El Paso in the late twentieth century, after having crossed the Santa Fe International Bridge with her daughter. Yes, that same bridge where Carmelita made her last stand. Doña Lola's daughter, Bertha Estela, your great-great grandmother, was the one with unusual abilities in memory and logic. She was one mind forgotten along the border. That is how you became a scholar born in the borderlands, how you jumped from the desert to 86th Street, and why you are now a citizen of Library Island. From that history, you emerged, a bridge between worlds.

We live in each other. Others live within us. History is always a new beginning, yet also a repetition and return. That is why you are here, Arturo, searching for yourself back in time through electrons in databases and musty shelves of documents, to this beginning, to what feels like a beginning, to write about that forgotten voice, to bring to life that forgotten mind. What happened to teenage Carmelita on that bridge that Sunday? Can you fashion these facts into a believable, living history for the newest refugees of Library Island so that they too can find meaning in their freedom and struggle? Will this history, even as half-lies, find a home in other readers within Library Island? How will truths on the page, if you are capable of such a feat, affect truth today, maybe spark a new revolution? What happened to her, Scholar? Who were you? Who are you? Who can you be?

Carmelita throws a rock at the gringo immigration officer who directs the small number of American troops around the bridge, and it hits him square on the shoulder. He winces and spits out more pleas to the captain in charge. Behind her hundreds of women from Juárez — some maids like her, others housewives who shop in El Paso, high school students, and even waitresses from the seedy bars — throw bottles, and yell, "*¡Ándale cabrónes!* Why are you taking photos of us? Why don't you strip, *malditos*, and we'll spray you with gasoline and other *porquerías?* We're not animals! We're not dirty! You are the disgusting ones! *¡Hijos de la chingada!* Shoot us, goddamn it! Shoot us, if you dare! Strip so we can see your tiny *chingaderas!* Cowards!"

No one is crossing the Santa Fe International Bridge in either direction. American immigration guards hide behind the windows of the clapboard bathhouses. Carmelita can see some of them laughing, and others seem more worried about this standoff, this spectacle. The trolley where Carmelita has been singled out and ordered to the bathhouses stands motionless between them, between the undulating, unruly crowd and the dozens of American troops and immigration officials on the American side.

Six hours ago, the fat trolley driver ordered her to get off, but other women rose to defend her. "*¡Pinche perros! Déjenla!*" The immigration agent threatens to turn the trolley back to Mexico—or at least to stop it in its tracks—if Carmelita and the others do not comply and exit the trolley and get in line at the bathhouses. The women call his bluff. Carmelita stands in the aisle and tells the agent to go to hell. Doña Cuca pushes the gringo, another smashes him with her purse on the shoulder, a glancing blow, but still enough for his blue eyes to burn with anger. Somebody behind Carmelita throws what looks like a jicama at the Mexican-American trolley driver, still twisting in his seat, and the tuber smashes against his skull. The women surge forward like a brown wave through the aisle. As planned, more women immediately take control of the trolley behind them and pound on the windows of the first trolley, screaming at the driver and standing in front of the green metal colossus and daring him to run them over.

The stubborn fat man yanks the brake on and pushes past the accordion doors and the women waiting for him, their fists pummeling his shoulders and shaking in the air. Pushes past the blows to his head and the kicks to his knees. He stumbles and escapes to the American side, his shirt pulled out of his pants and his *calzones* half-dangling from his *nalgas*. The immigration agent, however, has more nerve. He never turns away from the faces screaming insults at him, and he also never returns the few blows aimed at him, yet he wards them off. As he walks backward steadily and steps out of the trolley, this demeanor—his cheeks red with anger, his blue eyes fiery with hatred—keeps him face-to-face with them, even in retreat. Carmelita notices that the women, too, hold back with the uniformed gringo, push and shove him, yes, but never hammer him with closed fists as they did the frightened and fleeing, fat, *pocho* driver.

Seferina, a matron from Waterfil who once was a club wrestler, lifts up her skirt and flashes her already sweaty bloomers at the American soldiers, and waves her arms and yells, "Come on! Right here! What are you cowards waiting for?"

"*Ay, Sefe. No seas tan vulgar*. They already see us as animals," Chavela says. Both are from the second trolley.

"Did you take the keys?" Carmelita says louder than she has to. She is worried these older women will not respect her. But they also know her Uncle Pepe, and they know he is a veteran with Villa's *División del Norte*, the remnants of which are now hiding from the *Carranzistas* in the Sierra de San Andrés. Venustiano Carranza, that despicable traitor-general of the Mexican Revolution, one of many. Weeks ago, her uncle explained what he wanted to happen: "Get the gringos to come into Mexico, taunt them, and get them to invade and attack you. They won't hurt a bunch of women too much, but tell your friends to pretend that many of you are hurt when they attack, even if they only push you around and away from the trolleys. This will help rally the people of Juárez against *el vendido* Carranza, that American lackey. This will help el General Villa to reclaim his positions, get fresh recruits and supplies, and retake Juárez. This will help defeat that son-of-a-bitch mayor in El Paso who hates Mexicans and blames them for the diseases gringos bestow on their own children. You can help the revolution reclaim this crucial moment." Uncle Leopoldo pleaded with his eyes for her help.

"Yes, Carmelita, but—"

Behind the second trolley, a commotion. Carmelita struggles to see what it is. Behind the second trolley, on the Mexican side, she can see the Juárez policemen who have pretended to maintain order, but really have just stepped away from the raucous crowd of women and observed them, preventing others from joining the mob. These policemen are stepping back. The air is murky with dust, and already the sun has set behind the mountains and the shadows have lengthened. Some of the women are still yelling across the bridge at the gringos, but many have turned to Mexico, to the armed horsemen now appearing in twos and threes next to the policemen, to the grunts and whinnies of these gigantic animals, rifles and whips jutting from their saddles, their hooves stomping at the dust, these wild black eyes rolling in their heads in a ready panic. Dozens upon dozens of hardened, stoic men on horses.

These animal-men seem a different species from the hapless, confused policemen at their feet. Their skin is so dark it is almost maroon, dust covers their britches and stiff shirts. They look as if they haven't showered for days. Many wear bandoliers of ammunition across their chests or around their waists like belts. Not one moves without purpose, not one pair of eyes of these animal-men stray anywhere far from their commander, who has a thick black mustache, and wears a brown *vaquero* hat, an overcoat, and black riding boots. The commander is casually listening to the jittery police lieutenant. An eerie calm is what sets this man apart even from his soldiers. Carmelita notices that the commander stays ramrod straight on his black stallion as the lieutenant bends closer to the snorting beast and man and explains fretfully, gesticulating toward Carmelita, Seferina, Chavela, and a few of the others in front.

More armed horsemen keep arriving in twos and threes until a line of hundreds stands and shifts in place on the Mexican side of the bridge. For a while, the commander stares beyond the stalled trolleys to the American side—and then nods the slightest of nods. Some Mexican women at the edges of the protest begin to run back into the streets of Juárez, to slip behind the line of armed horsemen, but as these women retreat rifle butts smash the backs of their heads and shoulders. Their screams rip the purple-sky fabric of the cool evening. The horses shift slightly in place. Onlookers and street vendors also retreat into alleys and dusty streets and Juárez bars, to escape the chilly chaos. The crowd of protestors sways nervously like a giant undulating swarm of swallows. Three, maybe four hundred women still block the international bridge. The American soldiers reform a line deeper into El Paso, and lock the gates, and stand ready on the American side in front of the Texas-Bank-and-Trust-Company sign painted on red brick, dispersing what few gawkers from Chihuahuita and El Segundo Barrio have drifted close to witness the spectacle at the bridge on this Sunday night.

At that moment the armed horsemen press forward like an animate machine, advancing into the crowd, attacking the women with rifle butts, many of whom shriek and duck and flee. Their pleas die in the dust of the morning desert. The protestors break into small groups and desperately try to find a way around the animal-men. A few women sprint to the American side, and American soldiers yank them down at the gates, slamming them to the ground and dragging them away. Women collapse on the bridge, their faces streaked with blood, thick hooves a few inches from their bodies. Some are dragged away from the advancing line, while others are left behind and stepped over and lost behind the clouds of dust. The Juárez policemen push and punch women writhing on the ground, like garbage men clearing the human debris left behind by the animal-men.

"Carmelita!" she hears Chavela shriek over her shoulder one moment before a heavy shock explodes inside Carmelita's head, and the lash of a whip knocks her down. She imagines a ragged skeleton's head flying at her before she loses consciousness.

Carmelita Torres overhears the voices of soldiers outside the shack at an army encampment on the outskirts of Juárez. These soldiers are loyal to Carranza, but separate themselves from the regular conscripts with skull-and-crossbones insignia on their shoulders,

General Murguía's men. More traitors to the revolution, but these are particularly vicious. Carmelita floats in and out of consciousness, and her breath itself will occasionally startle her awake. Even if they continue to beat her… Even if they rape her again… If anyone, including her uncle Pepe with the remnants of the *División del Norte*, could ever reach her, she would tell them she would have stopped the trolley again. She would tell them she would have refused to be sprayed in the bathhouses again. She would defy those gringos who want her work but not her blood again. She would fight for General Villa and her uncle again…if only she can believe hers has been the first step to justice and dignity. But how will she ever know? How will she know what happened to her sisters and their brown children?

Her body is broken, her hands are tied to posts embedded into the dirt floor, and the pain between her legs feels as if a branding iron has been jammed inside her, and twisted, destroying her from within. She dreams of how it would feel to die, when the pain would stop its thunder through her body, when reawakening into this world would not mean witnessing their attacks on her again, their laughter in her face, their walking away as if she has never been there. Carmelita wants to will herself to die, but she cannot. She imagines one of these days beyond time…

At what seems like night, Carmelita thinks she hears other voices, but fewer in number. Those loud voices peel back a world collapsing onto her, this throbbing on her leg, her head pulsing as if malevolent fire-worms want to escape her brain, her breasts stinging as if cauldrons of acid have been poured on them. Has another soldier paid a visit? She cannot remember. How long has she been here? In another lifetime, she seems to remember an unshaven brown face over her, contorted with pleasure, with shimmery black eyes, a sunburnt forehead, yellowy teeth, his spit dangling before her eyes. In her nostrils lingers the musky scent of an animal that has smothered her. In and out of consciousness, Carmelita thinks she sees a strand of her auburn hair across her eyes. The curl and color of it shocks her like a fresh slap to her face. In another world the beauty of her hairstyle still mattered.

As she breathes the last minutes of her life, something strange happens. Carmelita thinks she can see dancing shadows in front of her and a hand in and out of the sunlight reaching for her face. But it isn't a hand from any soldier in this army encampment, and it isn't even someone from 1917. A man with wire-rimmed glasses, surrounded by boxes of books in a forest, with a distorted sketch of a woman in a newspaper— Carmelita?—and a photo of his grandmother on his desk.

Who are you?

I've been trying to find you. I…I don't know how, but I did.

How…how…did you get here? I'm free, I'm…the pain is…gone. I don't feel so alone anymore. I can't…I can't… Are we in heaven?

I don't think so. It's somewhere else. Faraway but it's here.

I think I'm dead. I want to be dead. But I'm not. I'm with you. Do I know you?

I don't know what to say. I'm glad we found each other. On the page, I hope, on this page you are alive. You are alive to me.

Is this what happens to the living? Afterwards? This purgatory? I was dirty, my body throbbing, I was breathing, but barely. But I did not give up. *Yo soy de la frontera.*

I am from the borderlands too. I am sorry you suffered. I wish I could have helped you…then.

I can't quite see you.

I can't see you either. But I know you are here.

I can feel you too.

Carmelita?

Arturo?

So you know my name? How, how…?

I don't know. But I do know you. You are from here. Wherever I was. I know you. Arturo.

Carmelita.

Are—are you in love with me?

No. Yes. I am in love with someone else. Outside of this page. But here, I only want to be with you. I keep thinking of your name. Carmelita. What you did. What happened to you. I keep thinking of you. You and women like you are the reason I live.

So you do love me, in a way.

I—yes, I do.

Don't worry, you are not betraying your *querida*.

I want her to love you too.

Can you…but am I not…how?

I want her to hold you. To breathe who you were. Who you still are. She loves the borderlands, but she is not from there. Here. Or wherever we are.

This seems like a very difficult task you have set for yourself. Maybe an impossible one. I am only glad my body is not in pain anymore. That's what I am thankful for. Can we love each other without our bodies?

I don't know. I hope so. Maybe I am wrong. Maybe I am lost.

Look, I never gave up. Never.

I won't give up either then.

Arturo.

Carmelita.

Stay with me. We need you.

The man surrounded by books stops typing and closes his eyes and tries to absorb feelings and images that appear and disappear in the ether like an orchid in the forest's mists.

ETERNAL RETURN

Vendo Claridad has not been back to Olive Street in decades. The first thing he notices is that the tabby lingering by the front door of Apartment One floats in the air in the recessed alcove of a small patio. The patio is shrouded in shadows. Next to that rusted, wrought iron chair where he used to sit as a child is Doña Lola's ashtray with three mashed cigarette butts. Vendo stares through the shadows. The cat's paws step in mid air, and its green eyes turn languidly toward him, as if to say, "So, here you are again."

As Vendo pushes open the black wrought-iron screen door and the hollow wooden door behind it, he sees Don José snoring on the rust-colored couch, unshaven, *molacho*, which gives more prominence to his tongue in a playful way, because who won't smile back at a mischievous, toothless old man who always seems ready with another joke?

"Vendo, you need to leave the dead in peace, *mi'jo*."

"I'm not disturbing him, señora. I didn't slam the door."

"All of us, I don't just mean *ese viejo apestoso!*" Doña Lola says a bit too loudly, which causes Don José to stir in his dreams. A silver sliver of drool dangles from one corner of his mouth to his leathery cheeks. "Come over here, next to the fireplace."

Vendo glances outside the window to the left of the fireplace. He notices that the willow outside is swaying to a gust of wind. This is strange since he doesn't remember feeling any wind on Olive Street. Thick, gray clouds fill the limited horizon to the Franklin Mountains. Why hasn't he noticed the weather before? When he approached *los departamentos* in El Segundo Barrio, no weather came to mind, not even the sun, whether it was morning or afternoon or evening, but now ominous clouds flitter in the sky outside and a chill surrounds the tenements, as if time is of the essence, as if seconds plop onto the desert floor and evaporate just as soon as they appear. Vendo slumps into his favorite armchair. His abuelita Doña Lola shuffles toward him, holding two steamy cups, but she places both cups on a small tray in front of her.

"So I found this special Mexican hot chocolate at Ben's Grocery. I want you to drink it, because it will help answer your questions, *mi'jo*." She slides one cup toward Vendo.

"I haven't asked anything, abuelita. I miss you so much. How, how—"

"I know. It's one of the perks I get from being on this side. I knew you were coming back, and that's so sweet of you, of course. You are the only one who still thinks of me, even though I'm just bones in Mount Carmel Cemetery with that sleeping *cabrón* on top of me!"

"At least you are together."

"Yes, at least that. He was a good man, even if he was lazy and drank too much."

"*Te aguanto.*"

"¡*Mira, mira*! You're just like me. As stubborn. As mean."

"Well, at least you're honest about it now."

"We couldn't have this conversation before. But *now*. That's what matters. Let me tell you about this Mexican hot chocolate. You drink it, you go somewhere, but I don't know exactly where. I'll be right here when you get back."

"Like a drug, abuelita? Really?"

"It's not a drug. It's Mexican *xocoatl*. With special properties. Definitely not a drug, but it helps you push through, through…"

"What?"

"Through…limitations. I don't know exactly. What it does for me is different from what it will do for you, on that side. I can only guess. We are not even together, you know that, right, *mi'jo*?"

"I don't even know how I am talking to you now. In Apartment One again. I write about you all the time."

"Veni, it's memories. The past. It carries you backward but also forward, but only so far. It's me in you. The chocolate will help."

"Okay."

"Drink it."

Before Vendo's eyes stop lingering over the soft wrinkles on his grandmother's face, which as a child seemed chiseled in brown stone, the cup with the yellow sunflower is in his hands, his grandmother gone. The clouds hover just outside the window—Vendo can feel the cold as if it's crawling up his toes onto his legs—and he thinks he hears the patter of raindrops and smells the aroma of the earth freshly wet. Vendo drinks the hot chocolate.

He is suddenly within the wall, part of the wall, and he smells the dust embedded there for decades. What is happening to him? In the wall, Vendo is half in and half out of it. Where exactly is he? Strangely he keeps thinking of Moises Fuego, an undocumented Mexican immigrant his father would use in *los departamentos* for cabinetry and brickwork. Not exactly of him, but of his callused hands, and how Mo-ee, as Vendo called him, would lose himself in his work. This wood now in front of Vendo reminds him of Mo-ee, the smell of it fresh cut, its rough, rectangular shape. The wood and Vendo's bones and their blood.

After another moment, Vendo is not with Mo-ee but with Manuel Lopez, who renovated his New York apartment decades after Vendo left Doña Lola and El Paso. Vendo is dizzy again, inside walls, seeing the metal frames Manuel uncovered after demo. Manuel found a decades-old 7 Up bottle hidden since the original construction of their Upper Westside co-op. An artifact from a worker of yesteryear found by today's *obrero*. Is that what this Mexican chocolate is doing to his mind? Time travel? Connecting one decade to another, one undocumented with another? For Manuel was also undocumented, also Mexican, but Manuel was an evangelical Christian, unlike Mo-ee from El Paso. "Manny," as the Irish contractor called him, had also spent time *"envuelto en drogas,"* but his wife had straightened him out with her religion. That was Manuel's sheepish confession to Vendo one day.

Vendo smells the construction dust inside the walls. Where are these walls? Has he traveled back to New York? He is thinking of the time he painted walls for his father's apartments in El Paso: Vendo also became lost in the work when he was a boy, lost in the smoothness of the joint cement after he had sanded it. After he would fill each hole, wait for the joint cement to dry, and finally sand the wall, Vendo would lose who he was too. Is that why he is now stuck metaphysically somewhere between these walls? There is a sense he is hiding in between these appearing-and-disappearing walls, his arm muscles and bones part of the sheetrock, his body embedded in the floor, a tile protruding strangely from his stomach… He can move, yes, but he also exists oddly inside the wall and floor. Vendo remembers loving to hide as a child. Sometimes his parents would search for him for hours. In that darkness, Vendo the boy would discover a solace that would escape him as an adult.

Vendo breathes, and he is staring at Manuel as he works on prepping the floor. But that staring is not in the past, but now as if Vendo is floating above Manuel, there and not there, like a phantasm trapped in his memories. *Mansito*, that's the word that comes to Vendo trapped in this nether world above Manuel. *Gentle* is a close approximation, but not quite why Manuel seems a kind of lodestone in this time outside of time, wherever Vendo is. Maybe more like *at peace*, as Manuel scores the bathroom tiles, breaks them precisely, and fits the pieces on the shower floor like a complex puzzle. There was a purpose that Vendo envied in Manuel, and also a connection to El Paso and *los departamentos* and Mo-ee, all of it prompted by Manuel's work on Vendo's New York bathrooms, these remembrances and impressions of his personal history. Now Vendo, the phantasm, feels none of that nostalgia at this scene. There is more of a coldness he feels, if he can feel anything at all, more like that joy at being invisible and embedded in the darkness he felt as a child. But this coldness is not off-putting in any way: he can see in a way he has never seen before. His arm moves within the wall, his finger suddenly separates from the sheetrock and becomes…a finger…

"Veni, ¡*levantate*!"

"Was I asleep?"

"Well, not quite. This Mexican chocolate is very potent. It took you somewhere. You are back in Apartment One in El Segundo, *mi'jo*."

"Abuelita, my head hurts. But you are not here either… I remember this chair. The one with the dark emerald cover and the frilly edges. Your favorite."

"I'm still on the other side. But also still talking to you. It is this special relationship we always had. We could talk to each other even when we weren't together, as I recall."

"I know, I miss that so much, abuelita. But why Moises, why Manuel, years later? I don't understand. Help me."

"Well, let's keep talking. It's in you. Not something I can impose on you."

"I don't remember you ever using a word like 'impose' in El Segundo Barrio!"

"Well, you know, the privileges of being on this side. The hot Mexican chocolate. Who knows? Not everything can be analyzed. Some experiences only must be felt. What do you feel, Veni?"

"A great sadness, abuelita. Mo-ee and Manuel. Once I was watching this show, *This Old House*, you would have liked it. And it has these men—I think they're from Boston, or near Boston—with great Irish accents. And I'm thinking of Manuel's Irish boss. He was a good man. Patrick. He treated Manuel very well, as far as I could see. And Manuel's work is still around me. The tiles on the bathroom shower I use every day in New York. The marble so expertly arranged on my walls, exactly as my wife wanted it. I saw Manuel use a laser-level to do it. Mo-ee never used that kind of level."

"It's odd that you're thinking of Moises Fuego. I remember him always with that smile and his crew cut. He was the one who used to be a boxer in Juárez, no?"

"Yes, that's him."

"Your dear father always thought he was a little lazy. Or a bit slow, anyway."

"Well, maybe he was, but apá also didn't pay him much to work on his *departamentos* either." Vendo shakes his head as he finishes this sentence, finally clearing his vision, which has taken a few seconds after finding himself in Apartment One again. The effects of the chocolate wane, but he still sees a forbidding wind outside the window next to the chimney, a wind reminding him of Easter in El Paso, the desert world somewhat inhospitable and pregnant with the ominous. "Both my father and Patrick used these workers. Used me and my brothers."

"Don't we all? No one is pure in that way."

"But that's not why I was sad when I traveled—or whatever the hell I did—to see Mo-ee and Manuel again. I was sad because their work was all around us, in this apartment, in my apartment in New York, and they have this show on TV, and all of the people who talk about replacing a roof, or adding a bathroom, none of them are mexicanos, with broken English accents. None of them have dark brown skin. None of them are the ones who do the work. We are still invisible."

"It's an American TV show, what did you expect, *mi'jo?*"

"And it's not even that. I used Manuel in New York too, just like my father used Mo-ee in El Paso—bless his bitter soul at Mount Carmel. You ever talk to apá on that side, by the way?"

"Haven't heard from him yet. You know…white Southerners used African slaves. And California growers and Hudson Valley farmers use mexicanos to pick the *frutas* we eat. And even mexicanos imported Chinese laborers and later slaughtered them during my time of the Mexican Revolution. It's a circle without an end."

"Abuelita, you didn't know this much, you know, when…"

"When I was on your side?"

"Yes. I'm sorry."

"There's nothing to be sorry about. You gather a certain perspective on this side, you become part of something greater, even if it's just *la tierra* at Mount Carmel. There's nothing wrong with becoming part of this earth again. It's only a 'defeat' from your side of things."

"Señora, but even all of that doesn't explain my sadness. I know all of that: we use each other. We climb out of wherever we are however we can, even if it means using others. Even if it means brutalizing them. Even if it means using them only to help us feel alive. Yes, that's awful and makes me sick to my stomach. But what saddened me when I saw Mo-ee and Manuel…"

"What was it? You can have more of the Mexican chocolate, if that will help."

"What saddened me…it's hard to express. What saddened me was this 'work' all around us, inside these walls, under our feet, above our head. The people who did this work, not here, sometimes invisible when they *were* here. Just like books."

"Like books? You were always such a reader, *mi'jo*."

"When I read a book it's similar to when I enter a house. I feel surrounded by the dead. It's a voice from the dead when I'm reading a book. I mean, not all of the authors are dead, but eventually… Just like not all the workers. But eventually…"

"That they're dead bothers you? It certainly doesn't bother *them* anymore. And well, I don't know how you feel about—"

"No, it's not that they're dead, exactly. They are. Those who are. That's a bit sad. But not quite what I feel. It's…it's…that they're silent to the living. I think that's it. Their voices, in these *departamentos*, inside the walls of every home, in between so many pages, in every library around the world—these voices are silent to so many of the living."

"They're not silent to you."

"The voices are there, but often unheard. Saying…but without listening…they become nothing. Reaching no one. A silence that saddens me."

"But why does this bother you?"

"Well, I guess it saddens me because the living, they often don't listen. They don't seek out these voices around us. They don't pay attention at least to the echoes of these voices around us. In things. There's this hubris in the living. Abuelita, you know what this word means?"

"Pride. *Orgullo*. Of course. I'm telling you, on this side, suddenly you are a part of what was, what continues…everything. So yes, even a few Greek words I know now. But I knew the word 'pride' before I knew it in Greek. I know what it means to have pride in your blood, *mi'jo*. I had it, and I always thought you had it. But wait…I still don't understand why that saddens you."

"It saddens me that the living don't pay enough attention, that curiosity is overwhelmed by exhaustion, by stupidity. That they waste what they have. That they repeat the worst of their mistakes. A circle of sordid history. At least sometimes it's sordid."

"But why would you *expect* that they should 'see' as you want them to see. As you do? Is it the expectation, is that what makes you sad?"

"Gosh, abuelita, what happened to you on that side? You've become better than some of my old philosophy professors. I envy you."

"Maybe it's time for more Mexican chocolate. Here, take another few sips and I'll bring more from the kitchen. I have to check on your grandfather anyway, and I have something warming on the *placa*. I'll be right here when you get back."

Vendo first takes a sip, and then gulps the rest of the Mexican chocolate. He thinks he hears a loud bang, and then a shuddering through the air, as if the air in front of him is a gigantic sheet of plastic that shakes, or is being shaken, by an unseen hand.

In front of him, Vendo sees himself as a ten-year-old boy. He is wearing a white t-shirt in El Paso, his *panza* protruding from his too-tight jeans. On the t-shirt it says 'Lee's Fleas' in lime green, with a silhouette of a golfer in mid-swing launching a ball into the endless white, which is now somewhat dirtied by a *churro* he is holding. His father and mother are somewhere nearby, waiting, while a crowd disperses from a public golf course in Ascarate Park. Vendo can see himself, that boy's face, there is something magnificent on it—a heady pride at having just seen Lee Trevino at an exhibition, at the cool t-shirt he is wearing, which he begged his parents to buy for him, at seeing his father's face so happy for once to be in the United States as a Mexican. As the boy Vendo is walking up a slight hill to the green, an Anglo couple descend toward him. The man, with glasses and a sneer, says with a Texas drawl to the woman next to him: "That's some fat flea."

Vendo the phantasm sees only black in front of him, but he remembers what happened next after that scene from his personal history. Vendo the boy was consumed with a rage that lasted until they returned home to Ysleta, in the Volkswagen Beetle, all six of them jammed together, Vendo elbowing his little brother's head, which, after a yelp, prompted his older brother to jab him in the stomach, which in turn led to a shout from his sister to their mother... Vendo wanted to throw the t-shirt out, and did fling it into the trashcan, but retrieved it and kept it at the bottom of his underwear drawer years after it stopped fitting him. He finally threw the yellowed rag away when he left for college.

It is unclear what this next scene is, whether it's in the past or the future, and Vendo is trying to make sense of it, trying to find where he is, what he is, whether he is. *He* is not there, but it's as if he's seeing the world through someone else's eyes. It's this Ms. Russell, and she has what Vendo wants, a certain fame or acceptance or attitude. She has brown hair and wears round tortoiseshell glasses, her skin is whitish, with the slightest tan, and her eyes hazel, but it's those eyes that see Vendo in a way he has never imagined himself. Does he even know a Ms. Russell? Her eyes stare at him like a doll's eyes, unrepentant, and in a way taking the totality of him in, as if to say, "Do what I do. Why can't you? What stops you?" Her face grins at him hard, with big front teeth just the slightest bit too big for her mouth, which remind Vendo of a rabbit, but also poised, with her big eyes, as if Ms. Russell wants to eat him. For Vendo, as he tries to make sense of the wavery image of this Ms. Russell, what brings the image finally together in his mind is her hair, this well-to-do do of perfectly coiffed chestnut brown, like a banker's or an Upper Eastsider's. This face, a mystery he cannot have, a perspective that attracts and repels at once, a chasm too far from his own face and eyes. Why does this image of he-as-seen-through-Ms.-Russell's-eyes make him feel so alone?

Vendo is trying to gather himself, trying to get away from Ms. Russell's eyes, or inside her head, or wherever he is. He cannot. He feels dizzy. What he feels is something very primal, as if he is leaping back in time, to the womb, and into what seems like a womb, a cave. Vendo hears echoes only, certain rhythms and sounds. He can see nothing in front of him, but he hears what he thinks are his parents, their voices. They make him happy, and when they clarify, when he can hear complete phrases, that soothes him—they are the songs in Spanish from his mother—but around him he also feels this chill as if a bear awaits the baby, as if without his parents singing these songs an animal will pounce on him. Vendo is terrified, but he doesn't remember any fight with a wild beast from his deep past or his recent days. Why is there this fear beyond the present darkness? *What* is this fear? They lived in El Paso. They were mexicanos from the border, leaving Mexico and becoming American. In El Paso, it was a there, but outside...beyond the border...what happened? He is *nowhere*.

Vendo the phantasm still cannot see in front of him—maybe he gulped down too much of that chocolate—but he can feel what is around him. That bear. That animal menace. A certain eerie, fundamental displacement, with a touch of an awaiting cascade into catastrophe. He is behind in a race he knows nothing about– that is what he feels. He was *born* behind. But no, *that* certainly isn't it. He is in a race where he doesn't know the rules and doesn't know how to avoid mistakes and dangers. Yet he has no choice but to race. He chose to *be* in this race, and that's the terror, that's the bear behind him, that's the fear around him, somehow. Vendo, in this darkness, is stuck in a labyrinth of his choices, and the choices of those who came before him. This labyrinth of many dimensions is closing in on him, approaching from all sides…he can feel the walls breathe him in. It is next to him. Everything and nothing are next to him. He reaches out.

"Abuelita? Abuelita?"

"I am waiting for you."

ACKNOWLEDGMENTS

I am grateful to Bobby, Lee, and John Byrd for first believing in this book. I have long admired Cinco Puntos Press, and now I know from firsthand experience why you are a great home for an author. Jessica Powers helped me to edit these stories and sharpen their characters and ideas; thank you for the care and intelligence you took with every word on these pages. I also want to thank the editors who first accepted these stories in different literary journals: Harold Augenbraum, Vicki Lawrence, Shanna McNair, Daniel Shapiro, David Dominguez, and Dini Karasik. I believe in the plurality and variety of literary voices, and one way to ensure this is to read and support the many independent publishers, literary journals, and bookstores across this land. We need those who "tell it slant" to nurture this life as a miracle always awakening with perspective and time.

I am also thankful to my sons Aaron and Isaac, young men who survived having "the toughest father on the Upper Westside" to become inspirations for your communities and families. In New York City, I tried to teach you the same values I learned on the border in rural Ysleta.

To Laura, I am profoundly grateful for the love and companionship you have given me. It is a debt I can never repay, but one I happily own.

*

Grateful acknowledgement is made to the following journals and anthologies in which these stories first appeared, sometimes in slightly different form or with another title:

Yale Review: "Eternal Return"
Michigan Quarterly Review: "Library Island"
New Guard Literary Review: "Fragments of a Dream"
Review: Literature and Arts of the Americas: "Yamecah"
Origins Journal: "Turnaround in the Dark"
The Packinghouse Review: "New Englander"
Hit List: The Best of Latino Mystery: "Face to Face"

CPSIA information can be obtained
at www.ICGtesting.com
Printed in the USA
JSHW012316120919
1451JS00003B/3